About the Author

The author was born and raised in Puerto Rico. He is a 1974 Bachelor of Science in Electrical Engineering graduate of Tennessee State University, and a 1992 Master of Arts graduate in Creative Writing of the University of San Francisco.

From 2011 until 2016, the author was an English Communications Adjunct Instructor at the University of Nevada, Las Vegas, and prior to that, performed similar duties at two junior colleges.

Contents

Short Stories

Lex

Not knowing why or when it came to be didn't matter to me then nor does it now. Some things you just accept without questioning perhaps because they seem to emanate from the expected, or because they are the natural result of things. Like my feelings towards Lex, for instance, who knows how I came to them? What matters is that they were the right thing for me.

Lex was as large as a grapefruit but firmer. It had all shades of reds and yellows intermingling to create an infinite range of warm tones highlighted here and there with furious reds. Its flesh was full of fiber and its flavor was bittersweet. I had the fruit no more than a few seconds before I got my hungry teeth into its flesh. There was so much of it! As any boy might do, I did not stop until there was no more. Then, I suckled on the pit until I fell asleep with my childhood dreams under the shade of the large mango tree.

As I slept, the breezes of the Caribbean Sea, full of the ocean smells and a little tired from their inland trip, softly rose around me, along the hillside, swooning the plants and trees and cooling the air. It could have been summer but, then again, who knows? The seasons in Puerto Rico do not assert themselves in the same manner every day so that the nature of any day of the year is more or less indistinct from that of any other. I only think it was summer because the farm was a place to visit in summer: a place to get away from the routine of winter studies, a place to pause, and to dream.

It seemed to be so far away from the city then—about 20 kilometers. The farm was but a few acres but nature gave it plantains, many types of bananas, mangos, yuca and other edible roots, avocados, guavas, passion fruit, soursop, breadfruit, and panas de pepita. Panas de pepita look like breadfruit but they have pits inside that are about three times the size of almonds. The pits are covered with the inedible flesh of the fruit. It is a job to take the pits out and clean them. But, although reluctant we used to embark on that task, once cleaned, we used to boil the pits with salt and devoured them.

There was a creek on the eastern border of the farm where crawfish that seemed small lobsters could be caught together with fresh-water shrimp and catfish. The fruits of the farm were too many to describe and too often, too easy to take for granted.

Sometimes my two brothers and I, along with some of our innumerable cousins went to the farm carrying nothing more than salt and a few pots and pans to spend a few days camping and having a feast. There was a small wooden shack on the farm but we preferred to sleep outdoors atop the soft grasses of the hills and under the starry blanket of the sky.

What fabulous dreams come to young and active minds! We debated topics like the relative value and possible meaning of Brutus' "It's not that I love Ceasar less, but that I love Rome more." Anyone of the troop could express an opinion—and nearly everyone did. We listened then. We had to. Too often what appeared to be the obvious truth turned out to be a mirage upon discussion. To see a thing from different perspectives is to see so many different things, and perhaps it is to see that in the end we only see a glimpse of the totality of anything. So it was that we dreamed. We had to.

The sprinkling of the rain woke me and sent me running towards the shelter of the shack some half kilometer away. When I arrived at the shack I was drenched with the gift of the rainstorm, a little cold but with the pit of the fruit still clenched in my fist. There were no dry clothes to change into so I took off the wet ones and dried myself with the bed covers and laid in the bed to hear the concert of the tin roof. This was a time for meditating and planning.

That was some fruit! It was a good thing that I still had the pit. It should be planted and watered. A pit from a fruit like that would yield a great tree if planted. People should take care of trees like that to ensure that they survive and to enjoy their fruits and their shade. So it was that the next day I cleared a spot on the western slope of the hill in a sunny place which had good earth and planted and watered my pit.

Many years would pass before I would see my fruit tree and remember this. It had grown to be a proud and fruitful tree. Its fruits were almost as good as the one that came before them. Although I had grown away from the farm and had come to forget the many things enjoyed there that was corrected then. I decided to buy a plot there to build a house where I would live with my tree. To ensure that my tree would endure, I would build a great glass greenhouse around it that would be attached to my house. I would install an automatic watering system to ensure that the tree would get enough water. The greenhouse would keep away the birds that ate the fruits and the insects that harmed them. And no one else could come to get the fruits of my tree. I carried out my plan well. Soon, my house with its greenhouse was complete.

Yet, somehow, it was not enough. Too many plants were sprouting inside the greenhouse and a lot of work had to be done to keep the area clean. To correct this, a cement floor was poured that covered all the earth except a few feet around the trunk of my mango tree. Because it got so hot inside the greenhouse, an air conditioning system was installed to cool the place and shades were installed in the greenhouse ceiling to block off the rays of the sun. The coup de grace was the installation of marble tiles on the cement floor. Now it was perfect. I spent many days in my greenhouse feeling full of enjoyment and lacking any cares.

It seemed like a paradise for about one year. Then I began to notice some alarming things. The tree began to lose its leaves and stopped producing fruit. It was getting in the way of my comfort. Why, even before when it was producing fruit, sometimes they were so many that they fell on the floor before they could be picked and stained the marble tiles. A lot of work and money was needed to keep the tree. I had to pay for the water, had to work to clean all those leaves on the floor and had to open and close the shades on the ceiling. If not for the tree, I could just leave the shades always closed, wouldn't have to pay for all that water, and wouldn't have to spend so much time cleaning up the leaves. It seemed to me then that the thing to do was to cut down the tree. I could get fruits from the store. The shades in the greenhouse plus the air conditioner would cool the air and make the atmosphere pleasant.

There were some problems with that approach though.

The greenhouse had no opening to the outside. The only entrance was from the house. Also, the tree was so large that cutting it down would create quite a bit of debris. It would be a mess to carry that through the house to the outside. One couldn't leave it inside the greenhouse and the cost of creating an opening to the outside of the greenhouse—if this was even possible without ruining the whole thing could not be suffered. This was the type of problem that my old troop would have enjoyed analyzing and discussing. Too bad the troop no longer got together.

Since I had to tear down the tree and there was no way to do it, there was only one thing left to do: sell. I sold the place for the first halfway decent offer and got out of there wondering where I went wrong. I heard later that the new owner tore down the greenhouse. He kept the tree!!

I live in a big city now. There are no fruit trees in my backyard. I buy my fruits at the market. Dreams don't invade my sleep now. Soon, when the memory of that fruit's taste, color and feel begin to fade it may be hard to see how some time ago I could have thought that planting and caring for trees was so important. Still now, in some disturbing moments, I wonder.

The Invisible Mole

Bobby was on the football team and the band - the only kid that played in the band at half time only. He was in the debate team and his grades were great.

He was looking at himself in the mirror, examining all those attractive features that had the neighborhood girls crazy about him: the blond hair, the blue eyes, the Mona Lisa smile on the full lips, the... Oops!

So, what was wrong with this hunk he asked himself: "Nothing." Well, not exactly nothing he thought looking at his invisible mole. Of course, being invisible, the mole was his secret. He had not told anyone about it. When he saw his mole, he was not happy. He only looked at it when · he forgot it was there and the cruel thing had a way of reminding him: it stared at him from the mirror with its inscrutable black eye. That mole spoiled an otherwise perfect face. It was a good thing that it was invisible.

- Bobby, I need to use the bathroom. How long are you going to be admiring yourself in there?

- Hush up. Can't anybody have some privacy in this house?

He opened the door to face his sister.

- It's all yours Sissy.

- It's about time.

He walked down the steps, past the living room and went into the kitchen.

- What's for breakfast moms?

- Nuts & Honey, honey.

- Give me a break. I've got the only mother who wants to be a comedian.

- Comedienne.

- Whatever.

He served himself some of the eggs, a couple of slices of toast, most of the bacon and a glass of milk. He carried the food to the counter and sat down to eat.

- What are you doing today?

- There's football practice early, then I'm going to the beach with some of the guys.

- Football in the summer?

- Coach wants us to stay in shape. We don't want to lose our edge now that we are state champions.

- What about the yard? You promised to mow the yard this week and it is already Friday.

- There's still Saturday and Sunday. I'll do it tomorrow.

- I want you here for supper tonight. Don't forget.

- Aw, mom. Tomorrow is my birthday. I am going out with my friends.

- After supper. Seven-sharp. No arguments.

- Oh, all right.

He went out of the kitchen through the back screen door and opened the garage door to get on his motorcycle. It was a shiny Honda 750 his father had given him for his last birthday. That was a man for you. Good old dad. The best dad around. Why did he have to die?

He got on the motor, turned the key and listened to the engine purr. He noticed a spot of dust on the fender and got off. He got close to the spot, blew hard on the fender, took out his handkerchief from his rear pocket and carefully dusted the spot. "That's better."

He got back on the motor, turned it around and was off. The California sun was high over the bay area. It was a cool seventy degrees. What a day! He took a right turn on Cherry, as he always did, and followed the road to the school. Coach was going off his rocker with these stupid practices in the summer. All they did was play touch football anyway. What the heck, something to do.

He parked the motor by the Oak tree, pulled out the cover and carefully tied it around the bike. When he was finished, he checked to make sure everything was all right before he started running towards the field.

The rest of the guys were already there and the coach was reading his raster. He heard his name as he reached the group and shouted; "Yow!"

- All right, let's break into the two teams. Today we are going to play the starters for 20 minutes and then we'll let the reserves take over for another ten. Let's get with it!

It was more fun than anything for the boys and the practice was over in no time. A new boy who had been playing defense on the reserves came up to Bobby and introduced himself.

- I'm Roy Mason. You're Bobby Hanson, aren't you?

- Yes. Do I know you from somewhere?

- No. My dad just got transferred here by your dad's insurance agency. He told me about your dad. I'm really sorry about that. The suicide must have been tough on you.

- What suicide? My father died in an accident.

- What?

- What the hell are you talking about? he asked Roy as he grabbed his face on the invisible mole side nervously. He suddenly shoved Roy with a stiff hand to the chest.

- Hey, take it easy.

- Woah boys. What's all this about?

- This guy just said that my father committed suicide -, He was holding his left hand on his face as he spoke.

The coach got in between the boys and push them apart.

- You're mistaken Roy.

- I didn't mean nothing. It's just that my father...

- Never mind that. It's just a misunderstanding, boys. Go on home now. Not you Roy. Take a walk with me, will you?

They walked a short way from the boys still gathered around their quarterback. They were all taking turns at patting Bobby's back and talking to him.

- Roy, Bobby doesn't know that there are some people that think that his father did himself in. He adored his father. Do you think there's any need to speak about this again?

- But don't you think he ought to know? How could he not know?

- You don't understand. Robert gave that boy everything he had and some things he didn't. I don't know if he killed himself or not, I only know that if he did, he didn't want his son to know.

- My dad's company paid the insurance policy. They investigated; they know...

- Nobody knows nothing! If they could have proven that it was a suicide, they would not have paid on the policy and if you're not careful about what you say, your father's company may wind up in court. Do you understand?

- Yes sir.

- Good. Now see what you can do to patch things up. That boy is very popular around here.

Roy walked back to the rest of the team and approach Bobby. A silence had taken over the group as Roy neared Bobby.

- Bobby, I'm sorry I talked out of turn. I got my stories mixed up. Here's my hand, OK?

- Sure -, said Bobby -, but don't bring up my dad again.

- That's for sure. What do you say if we go to Santa Cruz? My family's got a summer house there and nobody's there this weekend.

- Well, ...

- Come on guys. Sorry I got off on the wrong foot. Let me make it up to you. We'll have a ball.

- OK. Let's take him up on it. But I'm not riding my motor down there.

- You can come in my BMW, with me.

- All right. Let's go.

- We'll stop at my house and pick up some beer. My dad has a garage full of the stuff.

- All right but I have to drop off my motor at home. Follow me.

- OK

They drove back to the house, Bobby placed the motor in the garage and shouted,

- I'm off to the beach Mom. I'll see you tomorrow. And he was running to the waiting car, and on the seat when he heard his mother's scream:

- Bobby!

- That was close man - he said as he touched his invisible mole absentmindedly.

- Sure was -, said Roy -, put on some music. This thing has a great radio.

- Great.

He turned on the sounds and got lost in the music. He paid no attention as Roy got to his house, drove the car into the garage, opened the trunk and placed a few of cases of beer in the trunk. He was content to rest on his back on the reclining seat listening to the music and playing with his invisible mole. Soon, they were off. The one-hour ride went by easily and they were at the beach.

- Looking good, eh?

- She was OK but wait until I introduce you around. Say, why are you always playing with that mole. Isn't that dangerous? I would think that your folks would take you to the doctor and have that thing removed. It might be cancerous, you know.

In the silence that followed, Bobby was fidgeting in his seat looking nervously at different directions.

- Did I say something wrong?

- Stop the car.

- Why?

- Stop the car, God damn it!

- All right.

Bobby got out of the car, pulled a cap from his rear pants pocket, pulled it down hard over his left ear, and started walking off.

- What's the matter with you? Where are you going?

- Stay away from me! Hey, Tom!" He shouted at a passing car.

- What's up Bobby?

- Can you take me home?"

- You're the boss.

- What happened with the new kid?

- He's crazy. I want to go home anyway.

- Did he start asking questions again?

- Yea. some people don't know nothing.

- Yea.

- Do you think he might know something?

- No.

- Yea.

They drove in silence back to the house. Bobby settled back on the seat and took a nap. Tom drove with a wide smile on his face, looking around to see who was noticing him driving with Bobby.

- Here we are Bobby.

- Thanks for the ride, Tom.

- Let's get together later, OK?

- Sure. I'll call you.

He walked up to the kitchen door and saw his mother reading in the living room. He walked in and up to her and decided to asked her point blank:

- Mother, are you sure that nobody can see my invisible mole?

- No, son. Nobody can see it. But now that the insurance company has finally paid on your father's policy, we're having it removed.

The Wayward Way

He had just come out of school, fresh from the lesson about the men who traveled far into the northern wilderness in search for the origin of the mighty Mississippi. He was thirteen ("almost fourteen" he told everyone) and adventures were everything for him. To be out there, in unknown lands, living of the land: that was the life. As he walked home, he dreamed of someday doing what these men had done. And as he dreamed, he came to the creek he had to cross every day, sat down to take off his good shoes and, as he raised his eyes, there it was: the river.

Where did it start? Maybe it wasn't far. And thinking like this, he tied his shoes together by the shoe laces and hanging them from his neck, he started upstream. It was about three in the afternoon and the Caribbean sun was still high over the mountains of the central chain. The stream snaked along the base of the mountains, more a trickle than anything, barely washing the rocks that laid on the sandy bed and sunned themselves while the creek was low.

- Hey, Paco! - He heard someone call. When he turned, he saw his uncle on his stallion on the hillside.

- Hi Tío Ulises! What are you doing here? Are you going to the house?

- No. I'm on my way to see a friend who needs help fixing a pump. Where are you going?

"I'm going to find the source of this river!"

- You're going to what? - He had been nearing the boy as they talked and now, he was at his side.

- To find the source of this river, you know.

- I don't know. Do you know how far you have to go?

- No. Do you?

- You have to go at least 6 kilometers to reach the Rio Raguas, and that river goes another 12 kilometers just to reach that town. From there, you must climb the mountains to reach one of the highest points in the island. With a good mule and a guide, you might make it in two days. You can't make it on foot.

- Will you take me tío?

- It's too late to start on that and I have things to do.

- But someday...

- Sure. Come. I will take you part of the way back to the house.

Paco grabbed his uncle's arm and jumped on the stallion behind him. It was a fine paso fino mule. He was about fourteen hands at the shoulder with a coat of shiny brown-black hair that showed reddish streaks in the black mane and tail. He had been trained in that gait that was easy for both rider and mule. A good paso fino mule could keep that pace up for many kilometers without resting. It was the favorite of the big land owners but really too expensive for Ulises.

- Here you are Paco. It isn't far from here. Don't try this trip on your own again. Ask someone to help you in things like this boy.

- Okay tío. Thanks for the ride.

He hurried on to the house. He wanted to ask uncle Héctor what he thought of the trip to the source of the stream. When he got to the house, he dropped his shoes on the sofa and called out load:

- Tío Héctor. where are you? Héctor Luis!

- What are you doing screaming like that? You are going to wake up the ghosts with all that shouting -, It was his grandmother coming in from the kitchen.

- Hi Abuela. Where is Tío Héctor?

- He's at the mango tree. I had to ask him to pick some for Madrina because you were not here to do it. Where were you?

- I'll tell you later -, he said as he ran out the door to look for his uncle.

He went around the house and up the hill a few yards to reach the mango tree.

- Tío Héctor? Where are you?

- Who is it?

- It's Paco. I've got to ask you a question.

- Can't it wait? I couldn't find mangos in the low branches and I can barely hear you from up here.

- That's OK. I'll climb up there -, and he did.

- What's so important that you had to climb up here to talk to me?

- I had to talk to you about the source of the river.

- What river?

- The one that's down by the road I take to go to school.

- That's not a river, it's a stream. Why does it matter?

- I want to find it.

- That's silly.

- No, it isn't. Many explorers became famous by finding the sources of rivers.

- But that's not a river. It's just a creek.

- It is a river. Anyway, Tío Ulises says that it meets the Raguas river a few kilometers upstream and that from there it is another twelve kilometers to Raguas from where one has to continue to climb the mountains to reach its source.

- What does he know? It does not reach the Raguas river. That stream comes out of the side of a mountain about four kilometers upstream. I've been there. I'll show you tomorrow, although there isn't much to see.

- I see.

- Hey, what's the big deal. Don't get sour on me boy. Here, hold on to these mangos and throw them down to me when I get down. Then you can pick a few more. This is not my kind of work.

- OK.

As Héctor went down the tree, he could see the disappointment in Paco's face. When he got down, he called up:

- Paco, throw the mangos. Hey, one by one.

- Oops, sorry.

- You won’t be laughing too much more if we don't bring back some good ones. Look, this one broke in the fall.

- OK, OK. I'll get some more.

And as he climbed from limb to limb picking and throwing down the mangos, he wondered if Héctor was right. He would ask his other aunts and uncles. One of them might know, specially tití Juani. She was studying at the university. This made him feel better and he picked up his tempo until his Héctor cried:

- Enough, enough. Don't pick them all. Get down from there, you rascal.

And he came down from the tree with an easy smile in

his face and the hope to find that Héctor was wrong.

Later that evening, he found his aunt Juana sitting at the kitchen table studying.

- Titi Juani.

- Yes?

- What do you know of the river that runs by the road that goes to the school?

- That's the Roca Stream.

- Oh. What do you know of it?

- Well, it's runs downstream from these parts for a long way.

- But what about the source? Tío Ulises says that it comes from the Raguas River and Héctor says that it comes out of a mountain nearby.

- Hum. Well, it seems that I've heard that it crosses the mountain through a cave. So, it might go beyond that spot where it comes out of the mountain a little way from here but I would think that it comes from the Negro River—not the Raguas. Why don't you ask Abuela? She might know.

- Would you ask her for me?

- No. She's your grandmother. You ask her.

- Oh, you know how it is.

- Go on. I have to study.

But his grandmother had already gone to bed.

He tossed and turned m his hammock for what seemed to him long hours. He kept thinking of the prospect of the search for the source of his river. He was thinking that he really didn't want to ask his grandmother about this but he had to. She might know something. By twelve he was sound asleep.

He was awakened by his uncle Millín.

- Paco, Paco, wake up.

- What? What do you want?

- Today's the day your mother's going to call us at the store.

- Oh, no. I forgot.

- Hurry up. We need to start out i n twenty minutes.

- OK

- I'm going to hitch-up the cart while you get dressed and eat breakfast.

- Wait. I want to ask you about the river.

- What river nor river!? There's no time now. We'll talk on the way.

Paco got dressed quickly and sped to the kitchen to see what he could find for breakfast. As he reached for the door of the ice box, he froze.

- Don Paquito, what do you think you're doing?

- Hi Abuela. I was just looking for something to eat.

- Well, breakfast is over.

- I have to go to town because Mami is going to call me on the phone. Can I have something to eat? Please?

- Well, all right. But you must begin to get up earlier. There are chores to be done and we don't need any lazy people around here.

- Yes Abuela.

- Here. These eggs and bread were left over from breakfast. I'll heat up some milk for your coffee.

- Just milk please.

- All right. You say that Celina is going to call you today?

- Yes.

- Well, you be sure to tell her that we're taking good care of you.

- Yes mam... Abuela, may I ask you a question?

- You already have.

- No, I mean, about the river.

- What river?

- The one I cross to go to school every day·. Tití Juani says that it is called the Roca creek.

- What about it?

- Do you know where it starts?

- What does it matter?

- Well, Ulises says. that it starts way up m the mountains as the Raguas River, Héctor says it starts a few kilometers from here, and Tití Juani says that it might come from the Negro River on the other side of the mountain and goes across the mountain through a cave.

- But what does it matter?

- I just need to know.

- Paco, it doesn't matter.

Millín's voice broke through the ensuing silence:

- Come Paco, it's time to go.

Paco raced out the door to join Millín for the trip to the village. He did not tell his grandmother goodbye.

Millín was finished with the cart and was waiting outside the door for him. With a quick jump he was atop the front wheel from where a step carried him to the seat beside Millín. He felt the cart tug at him as Millín snapped the reins on the mule. They went on in silence for a while, each with his own thoughts.

- What is this about a river? Have you finally gone nuts?

- No! I just want to know what is the source of the

Roca Creek. Is that a sin? Why can't I get a straight answer?

- But, why do you want to know?

- What does it matter? Can't you just tell me? Don't you know?

- Of course, I know. Let me see. As far as I recall, that stream goes around the mountains for quite a way before it disappears where two big mountains meet about 6 kilometers from here.

- But Tití Juani says that there is a cave that carries the river from the other side.

- A cave, eh? Well, it seems to me that I have heard of such a thing, but I've never seen it. Where is this cave?

- You probably can't see it if you think the river ends there. Maybe you have to enter through the other side Oh, no! Héctor told me that he was going to take me there today. Now, I won’t be able to go.

- Don't worry, there's always tomorrow.

- Yes, but...

At that moment, for some unknown reason, the mule spooked and began racing toward the side of the road. Paco could see the road disappear as the cliff of the mountain appeared before him. He saw the stiff drop of the land and he grasped the side and the back of the seat as hard as he could. With each bump of the cart, he lost contact with the seat so that the only thing holding him to the cart was the grip of his hands on the seat. He saw that Millín had lost the reins and sat, as he did, trying to hold on, looking white as death and just as silent.

One of the wheels hit a rock and sent that side of the cart off the ground and Millín and Paco flying in the air. Paco saw the mountains, the ground, the trees and finally the sky as he was hurled from the cart to the ground. Later: nothing.

Incredibly, the cart was not overturned. The mule kept running down the mountain pulling the empty cart that went off, bouncing off and on the ground with the reins flying in the air.

After a while, Millín got off the ground. He was moving slowly, stretching one arm now, then the other. He twisted his torso around the waist and gasped. There was something hurt inside.

- Paco! Paquito!! Where are you? -, He called out as loud as he could.

He searched around for his nephew but it was hard to see where he might be. When he landed, he could have rolled down the mountain -, who knows how far?

- Ah. There he is!

Holding on to a brush here, a rock there, he climbed up to the crumpled form on the ground a few yards up the hill. And there was Paco. When he landed, he had hit his head on a rock. There was the blood. On the rock.

Paquito, he whispered.

But he could not hear him.

Millín kneeled, sat on his heels beside the boy, covered

his face with his hands, and started to cry. With a start, he felt a hand on his knee and he looked down to see Paco's half opened brown eyes. His lips were moving.

- Paquito! He leaned down to put his ear by bis mouth and thought he heard:

- It’s up in the mountains, very close to here. There are flowers and fruit trees, and a pond where the fish jump out of the water to catch the flies that come to drink. From this place you can see all four sides of the island. In the distance, you can see the ocean, and...

- Father, father! Come quick!

- What is it Nene?

- They went over the side! Come quick!

- Calm down. Tell me slowly. What happened?

- They went down the mountain, in the cart. somebody else. They're hurt.

- Jesus!

- Hurry father.

- Paquito and ...

The boy grabbed his father's hand and started pulling him away from the plantain field towards the road.

- Are you sure it was Paquito? -, Father and son were now going as fast as the mountain let them.

- Yes Papi. He was with somebody else. I was watching them ride the cart toward town when all of a sudden, the mule started running to the edge and took off down the cliff. And...

- Where are they? I can't see the cart.

They could see the road below them from where they were standing and the father was searching the mountain below.

- They're not in the cart.

- Wait, wait, there, below that breadfruit tree, to the right of that big rock. Do you see the man sitting down?

- Yes, Nene. Run back to the house and get your brother to help you hitch the cart and bring it to the road.

- Ok.

- Wait! You better bring a blanket and some water bottles.

- Ok. -, And he was off.

Roberto began to walk down the mountain. It was tough going down. There was no trail. The grass was still wet from the morning dew and a slip could mean a broken bone, or worse. He went down on a slant towards a tree ten feet here then reversed directions and went towards a rock five feet there and finally he was on the road. He crossed the few feet to the edge of the cliff, swung his machete at the tree before him and left it dangling, he cupped his hands to his mouth and shouted down,

- Hey! Down there! Can you hear me?

He saw the man stand up slowly and wave. He could see the man saying something but he could not hear him.

- Is that you Millín? - he shouted. The man nodded his head, kneeled down to sit on his heels and dropped his chin on his chest. " D e a r G o , " Roberto thought as he started to climb down towards his brother. " What's wrong with Paquito? He's not moving. If he's hurt, what will we tell Celina?"

He stopped to catch his breath and turned around to look towards the road. He could see the path the cart made from the road down the mountain by his kneeling brother and further on. They were thirty to forty feet from the road and just off to the right of the path of the cart. He could see Millín clearly but now he was seeing more than he wanted to see. A red rock, where the rocks were all black, next to Paquito's head. He took his time crossing the ten feet separating him from them.

- Millín, brother, are you all right? Millín raised his head to look at his brother with tears still in his eyes.

- Yes. I am. But poor Paquito... He's gone, he's gone.

Roberto knelt down beside Millín and looked at Paquito's face. His eyes were still open, his face was serene, he was smiling. Roberto placed his hands on Paquito's eyes and closed his lids.

- How did it happen?

- I don't know. We were just talking, slowly going down the road, when the mule went crazy on us. The dumb thing jumped the edge and ran down the cliff. We held on as long as we could, then we fell. Paquito... -, and he pointed at the red rock.

- Dear God! -, said Roberto.

- There is no God.

- Easy brother. That's blasphemy!"

- How could there be. This boy, he was something.

- **Y**es. A good boy. A dreamer and smart too.

- If there's a God, why didn't he take me instead?

Hush brother, hush he said as he put his arm around his shoulders and brought him close to him. They were still like this when Nene returned with Robertito.

- Papi? Papi? How is Paquito? -, Nene shouted.

- Tie the mule to the tree and come down. Did you bring the blanket?

- Yes.

- Bring it with you and bring my machete. Get the rope that's under the seat of the cart.

- Where is the machete?

- There on the tree.

- I see it. We're coming.

- Be careful.

He took off his shirt and covered Paquito's face. They came down the mountain two carefree, young boys, sliding more than walking, slowing themselves down by grabbing bushes and tree trunks, too much in a hurry to reach where they were.

- Paquito?

- He's dead Nene.

- Robertito, go cut two long poles to make a stretcher.

- But Papi, he can't be dead.

- There's no time for that now. You've got to be strong. We need to carry him up to the cart. Give me the rope.

Robertito had gone off to look for the poles but Nene was frozen looking down at the covered figure on the ground. Roberto reached out to him and embraced him. They embraced in silence.

- Papi, will these do?

- Yes. Good job -, he said as he let Nene go.

- Give me the machete.

He laid down the blanket on the ground and opened two holes on either side with the machete. Give me the poles. He laid down the poles along holes at each side of the blanket then he tied the poles and the blanket with the rope as if it all was a huge boot.

- Ok. Grab the other end, Millín.

Millín started to get up and screamed.

- Ah!

- What is it?

- I have a pain m my chest.

- Let me see -, And he started touching his chest.

- Ah!

- A broken rib probably. Can you walk?

- I can take care of myself. You take care of Paquito.

- That's beyond our hands. We're taking you up first.

And they did. They laid him in the stretcher and carried him up. It took them twenty minutes to climb the forty feet. They laid Millín down in the cart and did it all over again with Paquito. The boy was much lighter, but they were much more tired. The afternoon sun found them sitting on the road, by the cart, catching their breaths. They drank from the water bottles and just sat there for a while.

- Well, there's no going around it. We have to go back to the house. This is not going to be fun for you Millín.

- There won't be any fun for anybody for a while, Roberto. My pain I can take, but what will we do when we get to the house?

- It will be as God wills it.

- There is no God -, But he said it real softly and nobody heard him.

It was a good wake. There had been a pig, roasted in a pit, tubers and rice with pigeon peas. The cañita rum had followed the good one and the men had drunk. The women had cried, they had prayed, and again they had cried. They were out by the corpse with their veils on their heads and the beads of their rosaries in their fingers.

But the men were not joking nor having a good time. They were saying the stories, as they usually did about the dead in the other room but he had died too soon. They were remembering things that the dead had done. In a way they relived the boy's life through the stories.

- He studied so hard, that boy. - Millín was saying.

- What? - Roberto asked from across the yard.

- He said he studied hard -, said Héctor.

There was a silence in the gathering now. The last story had brought them to the day before yesterday. It was Héctor who broke the silence.

- I told him I was going to take him to see the source of the Roca Creek today, where it comes out of the mountains. He wanted to see that.

Ulises said then,

- It doesn't start there, does it? I thought it went beyond to the Raguas.

- We talked about it today -, Millín said -, he said Juana told him that it came through the mountains in a cave, and that from the other side it came from the Camuy River.

- He really wanted to find its source. Now he'll never find it -, said Roberto.

- The last thing he said was about this. He had to be delirious. He said that he could see it high-up in the mountains and that it was beautiful -, said Millín.

- Where does it begin? -, Robertito asked.

- Let's not start that up again -, said Héctor.

- But if it was important to Paquito, don't you think we ought to clear this up, find the source I mean.

- Well, we can all go over there next Saturday, for him. I was going to take him there today anyway.

- Go where? You were talking about going to this side of the mountain. What he wanted to do was go to its original source and that may take us high up in the mountains.

- I don't care how far it is -, said Héctor.

- We can't all go. There's work to be done. Someone will have to go for all of us -, said Roberto.

- Why not Ulises, said Héctor -, he was going to take Paquito."

- Not by himself. He can't be Paquito -, said Héctor.

- Why not Nene?

- I'm getting ready for the Farm Fair. I don't have time for that. Besides, I'm not Paquito. He's dead.

- Didn't you like your cousin, son?

- Well yes, but...

- Can't you see how important this was to him? - said Héctor.

- Yes, but...

- You can be an explorer, like Paquito wanted to be -, said Biembo.

- Why, you might sketch a map of the location and send it to San Juan. They might name the place after you. The Nene Point. It does sound good, doesn't it?"

- Yes.

- Then you'll do it?

- Yes. All right."

- Isn't anybody going to ask me if I will take him? - asked Ulises.

- Why wouldn't you? -, asked Millín, still speaking in whispers.

- What? -, asked Ulises.

- Why not? -, said Roberto.

- Well, we'd need a packing mule, a good riding mule for Nene, and a guide. We'd need money to pay for these things.

Silence again, but this time they were looking at each other.

- I could borrow Manuelito's mule -, offered Nene.

- How much will you need brother? -, asked Millín.

- I don't know. About a dollar a day for the guide, it might take two or three days and maybe ten dollars for supplies.

- About fifteen dollars! -, said Biembo.

- Isn't that what you make in a month, Brother Biembo? -, asked Héctor.

- Less than that.

- Well, we will do it, won't we? - , said Millín.

- I loved the boy well. Here -, he said, as he placed his hand in his pocket -, here's two dollars.

- That's a lot brother, but not enough -, said Ulises.

- Everybody, dig in. Give Ulises some money -, said Millín.

- Here's a dollar -, said Roberto.

- Pass the hat Ulises -, said Millín.

Ulises took off his pava and gave it to Nene.

- You do it.

Nene went around to all the relatives and friends.

- Hey Héctor, I thought this was a wake, not a stick up!

- Shut up and pay Ginorio or I'll tell your missus where you were last night.

In the laughter and kidding that followed, Nene went around gathering the money. Only close relatives put up the occasional dollar or half dollar.

- Here it is Tío Ulises.

- Thank you, Nene.

- Well, do we have enough? -, asked Roberto.

- It looks like we're going -, said Ulises.

- Great. Robertito, son, go get us some more cañita. We'll celebrate the trip.

- Hey, nephew.

- Yes, Tío Pepín.

- Bring the dominoes too. Your uncles Marcos and Ulises want Biembo and me to give them lessons.

- You couldn't even in your dreams brother -, said Marcos.

- Go with your brother Nene and bring the table and two lamps. These two want a chiva.

And from then on, the wake turned out more like it should have been from the beginning. A thing to let the living go on with their lives and to put the dead to rest.

The sun· had just lit a fire on the clouds from the east. As the mantle of darkness slowly disappeared from the valley, the figures on muleback became visible. They were hunched on their shoulders under the omnipresent dew that gave the plants and the trees a drink and the riders a chill. The mules tested each step on the wet grasses appearing to lean a little towards the mountain side on their snakelike progress to the top. On one of their turns, the riders stopped to rest the mules. They gazed at the panorama.

Ahead of them, about two-hundred feet above them and far away, the top of a waterfalls dropped the mountain waters three-hundred feet to roar on the rocks below where the Negro River began its journey to the south side of the island. Down the valley, the Negro River split just before the town of Raguas forming the Raguas River which went off to the East and continued on to the southern coast of the island. From the Raguas River, the Roca Creek appeared by the side of a mountain and meandered by the East side of the valley. A line of trees and bushes marked the path of the creek. By the creek, patches of plantains, bananas, and yuca interrupted the otherwise wild countryside. Avocado, breadfruit, mango and orange trees sprouted above the wild grasses here and there indifferent to their surrounding but gripping the earth with their roots.

From their vantage point, the riders could not see the cave where the Roca Creek emerged from the mountain nor could they see where it continued at the other side of the mountain. The mountain seemed to be relieving itself with that continuous clear cool flow of water.

- **How** far have we come Don Guido?

- I'd say about five kilometers to reach this height, Don Ulises.

- How high do you think we are?

- From a thousand to fifteen-hundred feet, Don Nene.

- Just Nene is fine, Don Guido. How much higher do we need to go?

- Who knows? This mountain is about five-thousand feet tall. I guess about another five-hundred to a thousand feet. That government map is obviously wrong though. Did you mark up the changes in the map, Don Ulises?

- Yes. Everything is done. We just need to reach the source above.

- Well, we better get going then. Let's dismount and walk a way to let the mules rest.

They got off the mules, and started off again on a slight slope towards the top of the mountain from which the Roca Creek emanated. Overhead, they heard the chirps of a guaraguao that soared above them looking for a likely breakfast. Closer down, they could see black and yellow reinitas, grey doves and multicolored hummingbirds flying from tree to tree to the ground in search of food and all around they could see the amapolas, begonias, wild orchids, dahlias and a world of other flowers that interrupted the green mantle of the mountains with startling flashes of color.

After a while, Nene and Ulises fell unto a rhythmic walk with their heads bent toward the ground, looking at the hooves of the mule ahead, with their minds set on the need to place one step down and then another and then another. Ahead, Don Guido had to make the path. He carried his mule's rein in his left hand and a large machete in his right with which he'd cut a branch or bush out of the way or balance himself with an extended arm as he climbed the mountain.

The sun was now high above them. The drops of sweat ran courses on their skins that ended mostly somewhere m their clothes but that sometimes blinded then or put a taste of their salts on their lips. The pavas gave them shade from the sun and the handkerchiefs on their necks, now soaked through, kept the insects away. Just two hours of this had them exhausted. Don Guido looked back to see Ulises and Nene gasping and said, "We better stop and rest. Let's go to that big breadfruit tree over there. It has a nice shade and the grass is close to the grown there."

The others followed him silently as he led them to the shade of the tree. When they got to the tree, Don Guido pulled out a large dried gourd container and said:

- I'm going to give the mules a drink with this dita. You may want to get a drink yourselves now. We will rest here a few minutes then ride for another hour. It will be too hot to climb after that. We'll have lunch in another hour and a half. Is that convenient to you?

- Up here, you're the boss, Don Guido. Nene and I will do the best we can to keep up with you.

- You're both doing fine. It's a hard climb for anybody. Lay down for a while. I'll give your mules a drink.

- Are you sure Don Guido?

- Sure. This is my thing. I'm used to it. You men rest.

- Thanks.

- Thank you, Don Guido.

- You're welcome.

Ulises and Nene laid down on the grass, beside the breadfruit tree and closed their eyes. Their hearts began to slow down their pumping, their breathing became steadier and their muscles began to cool down. It was over too soon, though, as Don Guido came over to let them know that it was time to go on. They climbed on their mules and started off again towards the approaching top of the falls.

- Here we are men: the cave where the creek sprouts. The mules are finished. Let's take their saddles off and let them rest for the rest of the day.

- Very well.

There was no way to go through the cave. It was too small. They would have to go around the mountain to the east to seek the creek on the other side. Come morning, after a brief breakfast, they started off towards the other side of the mountain. They reached the other side after a few hours and began to search for the creek.

- Hey, Don Guido, isn't that the creek over there? - said Nene pointing to the west.

- It might be. Let's go in that direction and see.

When they reached the creek, Don Guido said,

- Well, we need to go down to see if this creek ends in a cave to see if it is the Roca Creek then we can follow it up the mountain to find its source. What do you men think?

- Sounds like a good plan -, said Ulises.

- Yea -, said Nene.

So, down the mountain they went for a few hundred feet where they found the creek entering a small cave.

- This is it! exclaimed Nene. We found it!

Without resting, they turned around to follow the creek up the mountain. After what seemed to be miles, they tired from the climb.

Don Guido saw this and said,

- Let's go to that mango tree over there and rest a while.

They tied the mules to some bushes, and laid down beneath the shade of the mango tree. Two hours later, Don Guido suggested that they climb a few hundred feet to see the view to the North side of the island.

After a short while, a bid above them, they could see that the Roca Creek fall from what appeared to be a mesa. When they reached the area, they found the creek falling from a good-size pond of clear waters.

- Tío, do you think we could go for a swim here? -, Nene said.

- What do you think, Don Guido?

- It will be all right. The water level does not appear to be too high, and the water is calm. But stay away from the edge where the water falls to the creek just to be on the safe side. Just remember that the water is cold up here. Don't stay in too long.

As Don Guido and Ulises unsaddled the mules, Nene took off his clothes, laid them on a bush and waded into the pool.

- Burr! It is cold. It's freezing! But look, there are fish in the water, and over there, there's a whale of a shrimp. Are you guys going to stand there or are you going to jump in?

Don Guido and Ulises looked at each other and Ulises said,

- What the hey, Don Guido, I'm going in.

- Well, if you're going to start acting like a kid, I'll have to go in myself to safeguard your reputation.

They tied the mules to some bushes, took off their clothes and waded into the waters. As they splashed water at each other and jumped in and out of the water, the noon sun passed over their heads on its way to the other side.

- **Hey,** guys, look around -, said Nene -, do you see any water coming into this pool?

They looked around and got out to walk around the pool. The pool was more or less round, about fifty feet in diameter. It sat in a plain that had an amphitheater background of slowly rising mountains that went up to the sky three-thousand feet above on the South side. To the North side one could see the Atlantic Ocean and the city of San Juan. There were fruit trees and song birds in the trees that rose on its edge, and fish swam unafraid in the sandy bottom.

- I be damn!

- Don't cuss Nene. This looks like the place. Don't you think, Don Guido?

- Yes. The waters come down the mountain to gather at this natural pool from where they spill over the creek. It makes sense. I don't see any creeks coming into the pool. It looks like the water just seeps in.

- Nene, you will need to sketch out the view. Make sure that you show the river locations and the forms of the north, west, and east shores, and the mountain behind us.

- Yes. I will do it.

- Don Guido, can you catch some fish. I'm starving.

- Yes. Let's get some food in our bellies first. Nene, can you get some breadfruit from that tree, some plantains and some of the yuca I saw over there?

- Sure.

- Don Ulises, maybe you won't mind getting a fire started while I try to get the fish.

- No problem. Maybe we ought to get dressed before we catch a cold.

They got out of the water, dried off, and got dressed to do their appointed chores. They got the food ready, ate, and laid down to recover in the sleep the hard labor of the climb.

That night, they sat around their fire and looked at the millions of stars in the sky and t h e lights of San Juan. They listened to the tree frogs joined by the songbirds and the crickets in nature's nocturnal serenade that complemented the wonders they saw and the satisfaction they felt.

The Impostor

He had just read the biographical sketch in his desk and he could not tell why it was that the material had disturbed him. He was dressed in silk. The dark gray suit, the mellow red tie and the light blue shirt: all silk. His sideburns were graying gracefully but he still held that youthful look that made it hard for people to believe that he was already fifty years old. He was sitting in the executive chair behind the massive desk with the arms stretched out and the hands gripping the ends of the arm rests where the taut tendons showed through the skin on the top of his hands. He was staring through the panoramic window that gave him a view of the city close by and the mountains in the background. He saw nothing but the' cloud that did not let him see what it was about the sketch that bothered him.

The telephone startled him. He turned toward the bare desk to pick up the lonely phone and say:

- Yes?

- Mr. Delgado is in the lobby sir.

- Ask Nydia to go far him.

- Yes sir.

He hung up the phone, opened a drawer, pulled out the folder and laid it on the desk. But he did not open the folder. Instead, he turned his gaze to his right, got up, walked over to the curio cabinet standing in the corner and looked at the ribbons inside. Turning to his left, he walked to his four-by-fifteen-foot indoor garden that sat above ground-an island of nature in an artificial setting-three feet from the wall, underneath the permanent hale in the roof of the building that let in the sun and the rain. He had the garden built into his office to give some warmth to his environment, to bring a bit of the mountain into his office. He walked around the garden examining an elephant-ear plant here, softly touching the leaf of a dwarf banana plant there and sensing the rich smell of the still wet soil everywhere. It soothed him to be close to his plants. He had gone around the garden and stood gazing in its direction when he heard the knock on the door.

- Mr. Lugo, here is Mr. Delgado.

The slender man approached him with outstretched hand, smiling, carrying his briefcase with ease.

- Very good of you to see me Mr. Lugo.

- Not at all. Not at all. It is a pleasure to see you. I have enjoyed reading many of your unorthodox literary adventures.

- I am glad to hear that. Does that mean that you will authorize the biography?

- Please come and sit-down Mr. Delgado so that we can talk about it.

- Do you mind if I look around a bit first? I have heard so much about your office -, he asked as he walked over to place his briefcase by a visitor's chair - that I'm curious to see it.

- Make yourself at home -, said Lugo as he followed Delgado.

- It is incredible. All the plants. And what is this? The hole in the roof! The only office in the world where you might need an umbrella. What do you do when it rains?

- What do you mean?

- There is no glass ...

- The hole is to let the sun and the water in.

- But a storm ... "

- The transparent plastic hood inside the office keeps all the normal rain on the garden and there's a remotely controlled cover that is used when violent weather approaches.

- I see. And the plants thrive.

- They are in their own environment. They like it here.

- What are these ribbons?

- Prizes. Won long ago in Agricultural Fairs when I was a child.

- You kept all these ribbons but the walls are bare. see. But you don't display all the honors you have received throughout your life.

- That would seem a bit presumptuous to me.

- With the choice of views in the building, why didn't you choose the ocean view?

- The ocean has a mystical attraction for romantics, for the dreamers. But it is in the mountains that you find the solid ground upon which you can build character. But I speak too much sometimes. Forgive me. Let's discuss your business. Won't you sit down?

- Yes, of course.

- I have read the biographical sketch that you sent have some reservations."

- Please go on."

- If you are planning to write about me, I don't see are dedicating a whole chapter of the material to the story of my cousin Paquito. He lived a short life died tragically and senselessly long before I came into the public eye. What is your rationale far this?

Delgado reached into the briefcase, pulled out a binder and offered it across the desk.

- Here is that chapter. The only thing that precedes it is the introductory material. I believe that the story begins here. Would you give the notion a chance? Please say that you will read it and that we will discuss it again after that.

Lugo took the binder as his eyebrows reached out to meet in the middle of his forehead.

-But how?

- Your brother Roberto was very helpful. He told me how you and Paquito were so different and distant once, yet how you became so close after he pulled you out of the river nearly dead. He told me how your life changed drastically when Paquito died. When I asked him to, he told me the whole Paquito story.

- Paquito was my best friend. He was so full of the joy of life! And he felt there were endless possibilities. A strange thing in our time.

- Mr. Lugo, your life was no different than the life of most jíbaros until Paquito died. All you ever wanted was to be a farmer, and to work the land. Something happened when he died that changed your entire life, that took you away from the mountains.

I see -, said Lugo for some reason remembering the gathering around Paquito's wake.

-Very well. Ask Miss Soto to set up another appointment for next week.

- Yes of course. Thanks again far seeing me -, Delgado said getting up and offering his hand.

- It was my pleasure -, he said as he rose to take his hand while thinking that he could do with less of these types of pleasures.

He stood looking at the receding back until the closing door took it out of his view. He sat down and picked-up the phone.

- Miss Roble, is the governor in?

- 'I'll ask if he can talk to you.

- Thank you.

- Nene! - said the jovial voice.

- Señor gobernador -, said Lugo.

- Too formal far old friends. What can I do for you today?

- Bate, it's about the biography. Are you sure that we have to do this?

- Yes! I have three more years as governor. I would like for you to step-in then. A book by Delgado could be the key for the success of your nomination.

- Governor, I have given thirty years of service to the island. How many more must I give?

- Nene, you and I belong to our people. There is nothing else. Let's get together this weekend in the mountain. We'll talk about it then.

- Fine.

Lugo glanced at the material in the folder. He began reading the biographical sketch:

Introduction - personal information, family, etc.

Chapter 1 - Paquito's story

There it was again: Paquito's story - Chapter 1. He picked up the phone and said:

- Miss Soto, cancel all my appointments. Please call Manuel and have him pick me up downstairs.

- Yes sir, but ... "

- What is it?"

- Nothing sir. It's just that the afternoon is booked with appointments.

- It always is -, he said as he hung up the phone and got up to leave the office.

In the back of the car, after he had asked Manuel to drive him to the mountain, he inserted the cassette of Puerto Rican danzas in the tape player, turned the volume down and the reading light on, and picked-up the binder Delgado had given him. He opened it to the first page and began to read.

Paquito had just come out of school, fresh from the lesson about the men who traveled far into the northern wilder- ness in search fer the origin of the mighty Mississippi. He was thirteen. ("Almost fourteen," he told everyone) and adventures were everything for him. To be out there, in unknown lands, living of the land: that was the life. As he walked home, he dreamed of someday doing what these men had done. And as he dreamed, he came to the creek he had to cross every day, sat down to take off his good shoes and, as he raised his eyes, there it was: the river.

Where did it start? Maybe it wasn't far. And thinking like this, he tied his shoes together by the shoe laces and hanging them from his neck, he started upstream. It was about three in the afternoon and the Caribbean sun was still high over the mountains of the central chain. The stream snaked along the base of the mountains, more a trickle than anything, barely washing the rocks that lay on the sandy bed and sunned themselves while the creek was low ...

He lost sense of time and space as he traveled back to times long past and as he read, the car took him ever closer to the mountains. He had been reading for twelve miles when he came to the part that told of the accident. He read:

> - Paco! Paquito!! Where are you?" Ulises called out as loud as he could.
>
> He searched around for his nephew but it was hard to see where he might be. When he landed, he could have

rolled down the mountain-who knows how far?

- Ah. There he is!"

Holding on to a brush here, a rock there, he descended to the crumpled form on the ground a few yards down the hill. And there was Paco. When he landed, he had hit his head on a rock. There was the blood. On the rock.

- Paquito, he whispered. But he could not hear him.

Ulises kneeled, sat on his heels beside the boy, covered his face with his sands and started to cry. With a start, he felt a hand on his knee and he looked down to see Paco's half opened brown eyes. His lips were moving.

- Paquito! -, He leaned down to put his ear near his mouth and thought he heard:

- ... it's up in the mountains, very close to here. There are flowers and fruit trees, and a pond where the fish jump out of the water to catch the flies that come to drink. From this place you can see all four sides of the island. In the distance, you can see the ocean, and ..."

Lugo took off his glasses, dried out his eyes, and continued reading unaware that they had left the city behind and were approaching the base of the mountains. He read on in a daze until he came to a part that described the meeting at Paquito's wake. Nene's father Roberto, his uncles Héctor, Biembo and Ulises, and Paquito's friend Bate were sitting outside the mountain home talking.

- Go where? You were talking about going to this side of the mountain. What Paquito wanted to do was go to the original source of the creek and that may take us high up in the mountains."

- Idon't care how far it is," said Héctor.

- Wecan't all go. There's work to be done. Someone will have to go for all of us," said Roberto.

- Why not Ulises," said Héctor, "he was going to take Paquito."

- Not by himself. He can't be Paqui to, "said Héctor. "Why not Nene?"

I'm getting ready for the Agricultural Fair. I don't have time for that. I have to take care of my steer if it's going to win a prize. Besides, I am not Paquito. He's dead."

- Didn't you like your cousin, Asked Roberto?"

- Well yes, but..."

. Can't you see how important this was to him?" said Héctor.

- Yes, but "

- You can be an explorer, like Paquito wanted to be," said Biembo. "Why, you might sketch a map of the location and send it to San Juan. They might name the place after you. The Nene Peak. It does sound good, doesn't it?"

- You might as well agree, Nene, said Bate. They won't let you say no.

- The Nene Peak," he thought unaware of its blushing view in the distance ahead.

- Don Nene, you can see the Nene Peak up ahead," he heard Manuel say through the intercom.

"The Nene Peak should really be the Paco Peak, shouldn't it? It was his life, wasn't it? I never wanted this," he thought as a tear dropped down his cheek.

'Well," he thought, "it doesn't have to be this way." He picked up the phone and dialed.

- Don Carlos, this is Nene. Iwant you to sell everything except the mountain property. There is no hurry. Just do it.

- What's happened? This is so sudden.

- I'll explain later. You can reach me at the mountain if you have questions on anything. Goodbye.

He dialed again.

- Miss Roble, please let me talk to him again."

- Very well.

- Nene. Two calls in one day?

- But this is the important one. Bate, you're on your own. I'm out.

- Out?

- Out!

- What do you mean out? All of a sudden? With no explanations?

- Bate, calm down.

- Calm down?

- Yes -, he said with steel in his voice -, we have been friends for many years. You know me more than anyone. You were there in the beginning. We ploughed fields side by side. We dreamed of working our own land someday. Don't you remember that? Don't you remember Paquito's funeral? I thought that you, of all people, would understand.

After a moment of silence, the governor said,

- Well, yes. I'm just blowing off steam thinking about what I will do without you.

- You will work it out. You always do.

- Yes. What will you do now? To the mountain?

- Yes.

- I will follow you soon.

- Three years. And governor?

- Yes?

- I have a favor to ask of you.

- Anything.

- About the Nene Peak, I want its name changed to the Paco Peak.

- The Paco Peak?

- Yes. it has a better, truer ring.

- Yes. It will be done.

- Adios Bate.

- Adios Nene.

He glanced at the biography, picked up the phone and dialed again.

- Mr. Delgado, this is Emiliano Lugo.

- Mr. Lugo, this is a surprise. What can I do for you?

- I can see now what you meant this morning. But I'm afraid that this changes everything. If you are going to write my biography, it is going to be a story about how a lost jibaro found his way back to his world. I want you to be the first to know that I just rendered my resignation to the governor.

- What

- I'm retiring from public service.

- You're not going to be the next governor of the island?

- No. Let me know if you still want to write the biography.

- Well...

- Goodbye Mr. Delgado -, Nene said hanging up the call.

He raised his eyes and saw that they had reached his mountain home. It was going to be all right now.

The Father

- I did not pick my father. Given a chance, 1 might have picked someone else. 1 don't know. It's not that he's that bad, but for Christ's sake! The man should lighten up.

Danny had just had a run-in with his father and as he drives off in his dilapidated blue Mustang with the odd shaped tire on the front passenger side that makes the front of the car rise and fall with each revolution he thinks:

"So, what if I don't put the dirty dishes in the dishwasher. He doesn't either. He should talk to me! Why doesn't he look at the things he does if he wants to criticize?"

Danny looks very much like his best friend Doug. They're in their early twenties, they have long straight ash blond hair, they're slender and pale and they like rock musicians. Doug plays the guitar and Danny the drums. They want to start a band and they practice in the garage.

- Like the garage for God's sake! Why ask me to clean the damn place? He's the one that keeps buying all the junk and messes it up in the first place. It's every weekend. He says he's broke but how can that be? He's always buying things. Who needs another waterbed? Then he asks me to help him bring the things in and spoils my weekends too. And the stuff he buys need work half the time. The little time he has he spends buying parts and materials and fixing the damn things. And for what? Half the time he gives them away after they're fixed. He's crazy.

Danny arrives at Doug's house. Doug lives in a twelve-year-old California ranch house. The blue and tan paint on the house looks fresh and the lawn and the flower beds are well kept. Danny opens the unlocked door and calls Doug. Doug comes out and they decide to go far a drive to talk.

The young men get in the car and Danny drives off. "Hey man, I may have to leave the house -, Danny says -, my old man is driving me crazy."

- What did he do? -, Doug asks.

- Bitching about the dishes. But it's not just that. The man's going through some stuff, but what's that got to do with me?

- What going on there?

- The divorce shit, you know. Every time the bitch calls him, he loses it -, Danny says turning onto Thornton Street.

- Maybe you should give him a break, you know -, Doug says.

- Why doesn't he give me a break? I'm not the one pissing on him.

- Take it easy Danny -, Doug says holding on to the seat as Danny veers to the right sharply to get on the interstate -, we don't need to get into an accident."

- No way. How would you like it if it was you that had to read those stories he writes that leave you wondering what hell they're about? And then he wants me to tell him what 1 think. If I told him that, I 'd never hear the end of it.

- He writes stories? -, Doug asks looking at him.

- If you can call them that -, Danny says back slapping the air with his right hand. Like the last one he wrote. Here's a guy coming into an old town in the mountains where he finds an old guy and they go sit down in a hotel with four dead men. I mean, come on! Nothing happens but that the old man dies and the other guy leaves the place taking an old cow with him. Weird! And another thing, the man should act his age.

- What do you mean?

- He's fifty years old and he's out there on the basketball court every day playing with men halt his age. He comes home every once in a while, with stitches in his face or sprained ankles or knees. When is he going to learn he's no longer a kid?

- Listen, Danny. Cool it. You're uptight. You almost hit this guy in the left lane -, Doug says pointing at the white car beside them.

- Well, you would be, too. He keeps telling me to get a job, that he doesn't have money but, hey, he's got a big job with a fat paycheck. If he wouldn't throw money away, he'd have some money."

- What do you mean throw it away? You mean drinking and stuff? -, Doug asks.

- No. Like buying a baby grand piano when he can't play; like buying a few CDs every time he gets near a store. He's got over four-hundred CDs. When is he going to listen to them? And what about the TVs and the stereos? I t seems like there's a stereo and a TV in every room and cable everywhere. We've got three TVs and three sets of stereos components and it's just him and me.

And the beds, let's not forget the waterbeds. There's two queen size and one king size beds in the house and there's another queen size and a king size bed in the garage. Where's he going to put them? I don't know because there's only tour bedrooms and he's using one as an office.

- He did get you the van -, Doug says absentmindedly, looking past Danny at a dark-haired girl driving a red convertible. Like hell he did. He made me pay him back. I had to give him every nickel I got for six months to pay him back. Now he says I can't drive it because I don't have insurance and somebody might sue him if I have an accident.

- Well, all I know is that you need to chill out. Let's go to Berkeley. We can go to the park. There's always something going on there. What do you say? -, Doug asks.

- All right. But look, he wasn't always this way. That's what ticks me off.

- What do you mean?

- He used to be alright -, Danny says catching a glimpse of a baseball field beside the interstate. - I remember how he used to help us practice baseball when I was in little league. Why, one day, he was playing short stop and this kid barely taps a ball towards short. I mean, he barely hit it. Dad comes racing in like a mad bull, scoops the ball and throws it like a cannon to the black kid playing first base. You should have seen that kid's white face when he caught the ball. And the coach, he says:

- Mr. Rivera, these are kids here, you know.

- And you know, he used to load all my friends after the games into this old Volvo he used to have and take us to the shopping mall. After we had ice cream, that crazy guy used to drive us around in circles in the parking lot while we screamed and laughed our heads off. Where is he now?

- Hey Danny, isn't that Maggie driving that Chevelle? -, asked Doug pointing at a blue 1984 Chevelle speeding off in the slow lane.

- Let's see -, Danny says and speeds up to catch the car disappearing in the direction of Berkeley.

That night, Danny returns home around seven. The sun is still out when he parks the Mustang in the driveway. The grass in the yard is cut short to the ground and he spends a minute examining his handy work. He looks at the sickly rose bushes and sighs. They have to be dug up. The succulents look much better. He glances up at the two-story cottage with its sober grey paint and the wood shingle roof and thinks:

- What the heck! I'm going to have to go in sometime.

Danny walks down the short cement walk, unto the small cement porch, up to the French front doors, and into the house. He bypasses the stairs to the second floor that are a bit to the right as he enters the house, walks through the short hall by his father's bedroom, and into the living room. "There's the damn piano!" he thinks looking at the glossy black baby grand at the end of the hall. "And now he has to give it to the bitch."

The familiar room gives him no surprises. He has seen the wicker living room so many times before that he does not see it anymore. There is a chair at each far corner facing the center of the room. Next to each chair is a tower speaker and in between the speakers is the thirty-five- inch TV that stands on the floor in the middle of the wall. On top of the TV is an old movie disc player and there's a two-feet long row of movies to the left of the left of the speaker that nobody watches anymore.

In front of the left corner chair is a lounger and a small occasional table. In front of the chair to the right is a side table with a lamp. The couch is in the middle of the room facing the TV set and there's a coffee table in front of the couch where a huge book on French impressionist painters' rests. Another book on Picasso and one on flower gardening also rest on the coffee table. A lamp sits on top of the side table that is to the left of the couch, against the wall. There's barely enough space for the trunk that sits between this side table and the stereo cabinet that is immediately to Danny's left. By the stereo, above the trunk, attached to the wall are the tour foot wide, five-tier transparent plastic shelves. The classical music CDs fill the shelves laying on their sides on rows, laying on top of the rows between the shelves and spilling over the top shelf where you can hardly reach them. Danny knows that although the CDs look like a mess, his father has them in some sort of order that lets him find any CD when he wants to. Underneath the CDs, by the trunk, on the floor, is a book called *The Encyclopedia of the Horse.*

All that Danny sees is the man sitting in the middle of the couch watching a baseball game. He notices for the first time that his hair is turning white. The skin around his dark brown eyes is a maze of furrows. He wears a white long sleeve cotton sports shirt that has a four-inch- w i d e blue stripe around the chest and on the left side, over the heart, the word "SWATCH" is engraved. He wears dark blue shorts and tennis shoes. He is unshaven and his silver-streaked dark hair is a mess. Danny sees his arched back, his eyes reaching out to the TV before the once proud, now drooping shoulders, and thinks:

"Can this be my father? He doesn't have it anymore. He looks like an old man. He looks beat."

Danny turns to his right, softly walks away into the kitchen straight ahead, makes himself a glass of iced soda and starts to leave when his eyes catch the dishes in the sink. He walks over there, rinses the dishes and puts them in the dishwasher. He walks through the door to the living room, up to the couch, reaches out to his father, lays his hand on his shoulder, touches him softly, and says: "Can I get you something dad?"

- What? Oh, it's you -, Danny hears his father say as when he turns around to look and smile at him. Reaching out, the father touches Danny's hand and says:

- No thanks, son.

Danny turns and walks off to his bedroom.

The Thinking Buck

When the light of the dawn first gave a hint of its presence behind the slowly rising mountains that framed the valley to the east, Buck began to move away from the field of corn that had already yielded its harvest. He moved uneasily toward his hardwood forest home in the western part of the valley as if he were moving to get away from the light. And perhaps he was. Deer hunting season had begun.

Buck walked toward the woods with his ten-point rack held high above his heavy shoulders. The strong moving muscles ruffled the otherwise neat roan fur. The ever-moving white tail stood up right now, and his intelligent eyes were ever alert to every movement. He was the best the forest had to offer.

Buck did not know why the men hunted deer at this time of the year, he just knew that when the end of fall arrived, the hunters came. For a while, he thought it might have been something akin to the rut season for him, but it was late for that and that did not make sense when he saw them killing does. Because nothing made sense for that unless it was because they were hungry and Buck never saw the men eating the deer as the cougar or the wolves did after they killed. The men tied the dead deer to the hoods of their machines and took them off somewhere. It just didn't make sense.

He yearned to ask some of his fellow deer if they knew

why men did this but that would be useless. The other deer shunned him and would not talk to him because he was a thinking deer, because he was different. They were into passing their time grazing, drinking, mating and giving birth: surviving as best they could until it was time to die. They did not ask why things were the way they were. It was simpler that way. They just did as their parents before them had always done. They did not want a thinking deer close to them. He could not get close to them. He was alone.

So it was that Buck was stealthily moving from the corn field to the forest that cool Saturday morning in a Pennsylvania section of the Susquehanna Valley in what had been a mild winter, a cool December. It was time to play hide and seek with the men. For the deer, the rules were clear. They were fair game. If the men got a chance, they would kill them. The deer had to hide, not show themselves. If they failed, they would be killed and it would be their own fault. Buck was on his way to his favorite hiding place in a group of bushes that formed a dense foliage between a yellow pine and a willow. Men could not enter there. He played this game well.

For the men, there seemed to be no rules. Some of them got drunk and shot at anything that moved. In their haste to kill the deer, sometimes they shot themselves but they were there to shoot at the deer.

Buck cleared the last row of corn. He was jumping over a shallow ditch when he heard the shot and felt the burning sensation in his rear right leg at the same time. One instant later he was running as fast as he could. He felt the burning in his leg but it was not affecting his running. He had to run and to hide as fast as he could. The shot would alert the other hunters in the forest who would shoot at him too.

He thought the wound could not be too serious as he sped over the open field hardly noticing the crows that had taken flight to his right after the shot was heard. He reached and passed the old oak he had used to scratch off the velvet from his antlers in the summer. He was in the forest now, in the stand of sycamores that kept the sun from the ground and the ground free of bushes. He ran helter-skelter shooting straight between some trees here and turning sharply to one side now and then another there. He knew that this was the best way to make the pursuing men lose his tracks. He went past the lonely yellow pine that guarded the entrance of the thicket that was bunched together by the crab apple trees and the honeysuckle climbers that grew to form the dense vegetation he needed to hide and remembered the family of red squirrels that lived in the yellow pine but he did not see any of them. He heard other shots but they did not find him before he reached his hiding place where the climbers had taken over all the low vegetation and were reaching up to the trees and he remembered the sweet strong smell of the vines when their flowers blossomed in the spring. He had to kneel to get close to the ground to get through the maze of the honeysuckle climbers and the crab apple trees that webbed a nearly impenetrable barrier of interconnected branches and thorns to man. Through the race he had been painfully aware of the wound in his leg but he did not know that he was leaving a thin trail of blood behind.

He was thirsty and was fighting a desperate desire to snort and a natural need to pant from the run that had brought him to the place where his mother left him, after he was born, with the strong smell of the honeysuckle blossoms and the company of the red squirrels to go out to feed and to drink. He remembered his mother, the doe with the big brown eyes and the loving tongue that cared for him, that fed him sweet milk and slept next to him to take away the chill of the night forest air and he felt a bit more secure. In this familiar place he laid down on his left side to hide even more and to take a look at the wound in the right leg. The shot had opened a superficial gash on his thigh muscle from where the blood was slowly oozing. He began to lick the wound as he thought of the vagaries of life. He had been shot but just once though he had been in the open. The shooter's aim had been bad. If they didn't find him, he was going to be all right. They would not find him. The wound would heal.

Suddenly, he heard the sound of running feet approaching through the forest, rustling the dead leaves, cracking an occasional stick on the forest floor, stopping, starting again hesitantly, running again and finally reaching the yellow pine. From there, they started running again in one direction, retraced their steps to return to the pine, to run in another direction and come back again. He could hear a man stumble around gasping for air not ten feet away from him and as he listened, he remained perfectly motionless in the thicket concentrating on breathing easily in and out and on trying not to think of the gun in the man's hands. The man had stopped walking but his heavy breathing could still be heard in the forest coming from a place just beyond the yellow pine.

Buck lay listening to the man's breathing slowly return to normal. Gunfire occasionally raped the silence of the forest. He heard the man begin to walk slowly away from the pine tree until he could hear him no more. He began to lick his wound again though he remained alert to the sounds of the forest. Soon, one of the red squirrels approached to look at him as they often did with their unexplained curiosity. Buck turned to the squirrel and smelled for its odor but the wind was wrong and he could not smell him. The squirrel left and Buck was alone again.

And he thought how easy it was to die and somehow, that made him remember how it had been in the rut. He was not one to make a big fuss in the rut. It did not make sense to him to fight off opponents for the right to mount an un- known doe but he had to fight the instinct to do as the other bucks. But this past month, he saw a doe with eyes that called to him in ways he could not explain and something in him made him want to protect and keep this one for himself. And so, it had been. He had loved the doe. He wanted her to stay but she had left. The rut was over. She went off to where the does go after the rut. He was left with thoughts of the next spring and a new fawn.

The blood stopped oozing on his wound. Given time, in a few days, the wound would heal. Buck was in much better spirits. The hours passed; the day would soon be over. Hunting season would also be over soon and the men would go home to their families and to whatever they did with themselves when they were not trying to kill the deer.

He heard the squirrels playing in the yellow pine and he knew that everything was all right. He was thinking of getting up to stretch his legs a bit when he heard the sound of approaching steps from beyond the yellow pine and he froze to avoid being discovered. It was all right. He was used to being perfectly still for long periods of time and the wound hurt less. The squirrels must have been distracted because they continued playing up and down the pine tree. He heard them scratching the bark as they climbed or ran down the trunk and, when they hit the ground, he heard the rustle of the bushes. He supposed it was all right. Squirrel season was over.

Then came the shot. Buck had heard no deer. He asked himself, why anyone would shoot at squirrels out of season and how could one man miss him when he was aiming at him and he was in the open and another hit him when he could not see him? It was the right shoulder. The bullet was in his chest. He saw the blood coming out. It hurt. He did not want to wind up tied atop the hood of a machine. He stayed perfectly still.

Buck thought that he would not see the doe with the big eyes again nor would he see the fawn in the spring. He would not run with the wind again nor would he drink from the cool waters of a mountain spring. He would not walk in the cloud of a morning fog again nor would he smell the honeysuckle in the spring. He was thirsty. He had never been so thirsty. He panted. His tongue waved in his open mouth.

Buck thought that it was not good to be a thinking deer. That it was better to do what you could, as other deer did, to live or to die unaware. Not to think of the unknown that lies beyond life. He feared. Would there be another life? Would there be men or their likes? Did they have deer hunters too?

As Buck lay, he could hear the men leaving. After a while, he sensed that the sun was getting ready to leave too and he heard the squirrels playing again in the pine. He felt cold, very cold. He stirred, tried to get up and collapsed. After a while, a red squirrel looked in on him but Buck did not notice. Buck could only stare with glass eyes at the infinite distance beyond.

Paradise

Before the grasses took over the hills that surround the valley, the hills were covered with trees. There wasn't a single bare spot of earth on the hills. There were clear water streams in the dells of the hills where the deer came to drink and the trout hunted dragonflies while the otters played tag from eddy to pool. It used to rain in the valley. Now, there is nothing but the golden dry grasses that bend to the whispers of the winds that come from the sea to rise and to fall with the contours of the land.

In the middle of the valley lies what's left of a town founded by a young man who came from the east to find his fortune in the west and settled here centuries ago. A few bodies remain in the town but there's a smell of death in their faces.

It is a small town. Even when it was the supply center for the timber crews that clear-cut the forests of the hills, the town was small. The streets are unpaved and here and there some grasses try to reclaim them. Elm, the main street, runs nine-hundred feet from the south to the north bisecting South and North. These are streets that run parallel to each other, some sixty-feet apart. North Street, the smaller of the three streets, is one-hundred feet from the north end of Elm.

One spring day, Paul reached the top of the hills that surround the valley to the South. Paul was a veteran who had been shot three times and had lost his best friends in the war. Now, he went from place to place seeking the peace of mind that the war took away from him. He was only twenty-four, but he thought he was through with society, with life. He was six feet tall, had wide shoulders, black hair and eyes, and features that seemed to come from a foreign land. His face was pale. He let his black curly hair grow long to his shoulders and his full beard covered most of his face. He was dressed to walk in the hills with a backpack that rose above the black baseball cap he wore on his head. He wore a plaid red and white heavy cotton shirt, pale blue jeans and strong black walking boots. He walked carrying a six-foot long staff that he swung to a spot on the ground ahead of him, letting it rest there until he caught up with the spot before he swung it ahead again.

Paul looked down on the town to see the patriarchal cross made by the streets of the town and thought: "Maybe here, away from the crowd and the cars and the constant fight for survival I will find peace. We'll see."

It was in mid-morning and the day was cool and the sun was shining in the cloudless sky. The mist of the morning was still on the leaves of the grasses and the black boots had collected the mist in droplets of water. Paul came down from the mountain to the town. At the beginning of Elm Street were two poles- one at each side of the street that held up the ropes tied to the hardly legible sign that swayed in the wind: Paradise.

He could see that the houses were crumbling in ever languid slow motion. Their wood was raw. With the passing years, it had turned to the color of a grayish earth. The lots were covered with the same grasses that covered the hills, and here and there, a tumbleweed rolled along an empty street.

Paul walked up Elm looking at the houses and at the signs

of the businesses that barely hung to the ropes that kept them swinging in the air. "It's a dead town," he thought. "Except for some ghosts, there can be no one here. Too bad. A bath and a bed would have been good. But maybe there is still a well." He climbed to the east side sidewalk of Elm and the squeaking sound of complaining wood began to follow his boots.

When he reached South Street, a Rhode Island red hen flew out of an open door with a flapper of wings and a cackling racket and landed in front of him to walk away from him, on the sidewalk, complaining. Paul was a statue staring at the hen when the slender bent down figure of the man came out of the same door holding a broom and saying:

- You stay out of here, you vermin. You're not welcomed here.

Paul thought that he surely was addressing the hen and called out to the man:

- Good morning, sir!

The man spun around to point his chin at Paul and examined him through squinted eyelids.

- And who may you be, sir?

Paul told him who he was and that he was glad that the town was not deserted as he first thought. To this the man said:

- It's deserted enough, it's in a desert and there are no deserts here. No, sir. That's what we've gone to. Just a few of us remain. What are you doing here?

- I've been wandering in these mountains for several days. This morning I reached the crest of that mountain -, Paul said pointing to the South -, and there you were. - Paul looked at the old man trying to guess his age and guessed seventy.

- Well, you're welcome to stay to rest your legs before you're welcome to go on wandering somewhere else. There's nothing here for you. Follow me and I'll show you to the hotel. The others are there -, said the old man and he started walking away from Paul to the north.

Paul followed as the man slowly crossed South Street and began moving on Elm towards North Street.

- Say, what is your name sir? - asked Paul.

- Name is Thomas, Thomas Manfield. And here we are -, he said as he turned to open the door of the first building on the east side of Elm Street between South and North streets.

- The rest are here.

Paul followed the man through the open door into the dark room and stood just beyond the door for a moment to let his eyes get used to the darkness. After a while, he could see that they had entered the lobby of an old hotel. The ceilings were eleven feet high. Although it was warm enough outside, it was cold in here. The front windows and the glass on the door were covered with heavy drapes. He could see ahead to his right the registration desk with the large open register. Above the desk was the single oil lamp that was shedding light in the room. By the side of the register was the pen holder. There was no pen. To the left, against the wall behind the desk was the grandfather clock that made the only sound that was heard. A dull tick, tick, tick. Beyond the desk to the right were the stairs that led to the rooms upstairs. The bare walls were covered with dust. There was a musty smell in the air. He turned to his left to see a large sitting room in which there were a number of chairs in the shadows. After a while he began to see that there were five Queen Ann chairs in various stages of disrepair arranged in a semicircle facing away from him. He could see the faint outline of heads and hats and hair above the backrests of the chairs and could hear the voice of Thomas Manfield calling out to him:

- We're over here. Come and join us. Bring the chair behind the desk.

Paul went and got the straight wooden chair and took it with him as he walked over to join the citizens of Paradise. He placed the chair facing the sat down trying to see the faces. It was very dark in that part of the room and Paul, looking into the light of the oil lamp, could not quite make out the faces in the chairs. He could see that there was no movement anywhere.

- Don't mind them. They don't say anything. They just sit here. They keep me company. It is good to have company. Like this I mean. No arguments. I used to think that silence was bad. But no. No. Silence is good. There is no argument in silence. No sir. Just peace.

Paul felt cold in the wooden chair looking at the faces in the shadows and as he got used to the dark, he began to see details in the faces. There, to his left was the figure with the hat that fell too far down the face hiding the eyes but not no Paul thought, not the hole in the face where the mouth should have been and not the teeth without lips and the jaw that fell to hang in the air above his chest. He was dead. Not a cadaver. A skeleton. Dead. Dressed. Sitting there. He looked at the rest of them and one by one he saw: they were the same. All. Except Thomas Manfield. Thomas sat last of all. Facing him. Unsmiling. Thomas said:

- You rest here. Talk to them if you want. They listen

well. No interruptions. No. I must be off to get some water from the well. There is one more body in the town to take care of. I won't be long.

- Mr. Manfield -, Paul said hurriedly as the faint moo of a cow was heard across the open door of the hotel where Mr. Manfield was standing -, just a minute.

- Yes?

- I am thirsty, perhaps I will come along and get water from the well.

- Come along then.

Paul followed Thomas Manfield out of the building into the heat of the day and they walked north on Elm to North Street where they crossed the street and followed North to its west end to get to the well. They walked in silence but Paul was full of questions he wanted to but dared not ask. He thought: "Was this man mad? He had to be. All the dead. Unburied. Sitting there. Why were they there? Were there any more dead around? How did they die? Who were they? Who was this man?"

Paul examined Thomas Manfield again to see him for the first time in the open sun. Thomas was wearing a weathered hat with a brim and a crown that had lost their original shapes long ago. They now undulated haphazardly in awkward inconsistent waves. His eyes were a consistent set of straight slits atop the half-glasses that sat precariously on the end of his slightly turned up nose. You could not see the eyes. But around the eyes and in the rest of his face you could see the scars that the years had left on his skin. Below the nose was the mouth with the thin lips that had not smiled and that puckered out once in a while with what seemed to be an involuntary twitch or an unconscious habit that had a rhythm of its own. He wore cotton in the tan coat, the blue pants and the shirt that once was white but now looked like old cream; and brown leather in the boots and the belt and the buttons of the coat that hung loose from their holding threads. The clothes also hung loose on his shoulders and his neck could not hope to fill the neck of the shirt. At his waist, the tip of the belt hung a foot beyond the keeper, and beyond the neat punch-holes on the panel of the belt was an odd succession of dissimilar holes that somehow seemed to travel inexorably toward the frame.

- Eighty-four years old. That's what I am -, said Thomas when they got to the well. He lowered the bucket in the well and drew water, gave Paul a tin cup full and said:

- Not a day older yesterday. Tell.me, how did you like my Presbyterians friends? They're something aren't they?

- Mr. Manfield...

- Thomas. It's just you and me.

- Thomas. Who were they?

- They were the town people. I should be resting with them too but I'm too stubborn. Must be the Highlander blood in me. Each spring the garden yields less. The seed. It may be the seed. But how do you plow the land with these arms? -, he said raising the frail things to Paul. "The chickens and the pigs have grown wild. The cow grows old. Soon I will join the hotel crowd. To rest my mind. It used to be that I could work from sunup to sunset, day after day after day. No more. You should have seen it -, said Thomas arching a hand in a semicircle to the north -, when there were forests in the mountains. We cut timber. There are no more forests. It's a miracle. There have been no fires. But soon. The cow's milk will dry-up and so will the well and the garden will tire of yielding and yielding. Or maybe a fire. But it's all right I guess -, Thomas said with a pleading hand -, what else is there now?

- What happened to them? - asked Paul still holding the tin drinking cup.

Thomas was leaning against the fence of the well looking out to the lazy slopes of the hills beyond. He turned to look at Paul and said:

- They got tired and quit. The owner of the hotel was the first one. I found him on his chair and I was too busy trying to feed and to care for the rest of them so I just left him there. I mean, I couldn't dig a proper grave for him and no one was using the hotel. They began to quit on me and all of them sickly and just me and I just carried them in the wheelbarrow one by one as they quit on me to the hotel and they kept each other company and they rested there fine. Now, they're all there. The last one, the barkeeper, got there five years ago last February. I will join them soon.

- What about the women? Weren't there any women? -, asked Paul as he walked to the other side of the well across from Thomas to lean on the rail of the well.

- Yes -, replied Thomas -, but they're in the warehouse. It did not seem proper to leave them in public sight with the men. No privacy like that you know. They're more comfortable by themselves in the warehouse. Nobody ever goes there.

- How many?

- Who knows? Three or four. I don't remember. I did the

best I could. They died. Now we, the men, we rest in the hotel. The women are in the warehouse. I do the chores that keep me alive. I put water in the trough for the cow. I milk the cow. I irrigate the garden. I eat. I sleep- sometimes. That's all.

Paul thought about that. The man's mind seemed sound. But there was something missing that Paul could not fathom. No. Everyone had died around him. He had spent five years by himself among the dead. How do you recover from that? He had to be insane.

- You think me a looney perhaps? -, asked Thomas looking straight into Paul's open black eyes.

- No -, said Paul -, I was thinking about what you said. You do what you must to survive. That's all.

- So?

Paul could not bring himself to say that he was wondering why he went through the trouble. There wasn't much to live far here.

- Why do you do it? - he realized he had asked out loud when he heard Thomas say:

- I've often wondered that myself. Why go through the trouble? What is to be gained from another day no different from any other day already experienced and me none the better for it. The days pass like the movements of the pendulum of the clock in the hotel. Sometimes moving one way, sometimes the other, but just marking the passage of time.

- Tell me Thomas, who were those people? - asked Paul.

- The hotel man, the barkeeper, the judge, the doctor: each

one a dreamer whose dream did not come through. The hotel man had high hopes of owning a big city hotel, you know, with the big shows and the gambling maybe. The barkeeper never did say what he never got. He was a private man but you could tell that there was something eating him up. Here -, Thomas said, handing Paul a bucket of water -, you don't mind carrying it do you? Let's walk back. - And he started off in the middle of the street with Paul beside him.

- The judge wanted to study law. He was the closest thing we had here to the law. He settled our differences so we called him judge. He never got to study law or anything else for that matter. The doctor was very much like the judge. He was a smart man. He read all he could find about medicine but he was no doctor. He did the best he could. Dreams that did not come through ...

- And you? – asked Paul looking at him as they walked the dusty street.

- Me? You'll not catch me dreaming. I've seen what that does to a man. Breaking him up inside as the days go by and the hope dies little by little. No sir! Not for me. I bide my time, live my days 'till it's time for me to rest. I'll join them in the hotel when my time comes.

- You never had a dream? Something that you really wanted? Something that you had to have no matter what? -, Asked Paul.

Thomas stopped in the middle of the street and tried as best as he could to straighten up his body, took a deep breath and said:

- Dreams are for children. A grown-up man does not dream. Enough of this! You would have me bare my soul to you? A stranger?

Paul looked down on Thomas and tried to calm him.

- I'm sorry Thomas. I didn't mean to pry.

- Sorry? You come out of nowhere asking all these questions and breaking the peace, and that's what you've got to say?

- What else can I say, Thomas?

Thomas turned away from Paul and began walking again. Paul followed Thomas at a distance. As Thomas walked away, Paul could hear him mumbling to himself. But in a few seconds, he seemed to calm down and became quiet. Soon, they were at the hotel. Thomas reached out for the column on the sidewalk and leaned on it. He stayed there resting it seemed to Paul for a moment but when he tried to step up to the sidewalk, he slipped and fell. Paul was too slow to catch him and Thomas landed face down on the sidewalk. Paul laid down the bucket of water and hurried to his side.

- Thomas! -, Paul said, grabbing him and turning him gingerly.

Thomas raised his right arm trying to sit up and Paul put his left arm around his shoulders and pulled him up. There was a trickle of blood running down the side of Thomas' face. Its red contrasted with the flesh that had lost all its blood in the fall.

- Are you all right? -, asked Paul.

- All right? No. Take me inside. To my chair. With the others.

Paul picked him up and carried him through the door, to his chair and set him down carefully. He kneeled down beside him and said:

- Look, I'm awfully sorry I upset you. Please tell me you're going to be all right.

- Don't you worry Paul. You've only been here a couple of hours. I've been living eighty-four years. It's life. Not you.

- But if I hadn't ...

- Be quiet for a minute -, said Thomas, searching for breath and placing his right hand on Paul's shoulder. - I must tell you that I too had a dream. I've told this to no one. Everyone thought that I was a rock. No flesh here. Solid rock. But a man is not a rock -, Thomas said squeezing Paul's shoulder with surprising strength.

- Don't talk. Just rest. Please. Just take it easy. What can I get you? -, said Paul looking around the room.

- There is nothing -, said Thomas. - Listen, I must talk about this dream. I must share this with you before I join my friends here or I won't be able to rest with them.

- All right. But take your time. Don't get excited -, said Paul.

- Years ago, I was a cutter in the forest. I helped turn the most beautiful place on earth to grass and dust. I did it for money. Now, and since I first got up one morning a few years back to see, to really see, for the first time, what we did to the hills, I have this dream of turning it back. Of putting it all back like it was in the beginning. I started, you see, I planted a couple of apple trees in the garden beyond the well. They don't do well. I wanted to see the trees come back to the hills; I wanted to see the birds and the deer and the streams ...

- Thomas -, Paul cried out when he saw Thomas' eyes close.

After a while, Thomas opened his eyes and said:

- Yes. It is too late for me. And you Paul, what are you doing in Paradise?

*** *** ***

The next day, Paul finished the last of the graves he dug just north of the well. There were no flowers to lay on the graves but he covered them with rocks. He looked at his work. There was the doctor, the judge, the barkeeper, the innkeeper and Thomas. He buried the women to the south of town. Thomas seemed to want it so.

He thought about saying a prayer but couldn't. Instead, he went to the well and washed his face and his hands. Then, he put on his backpack and picked up his staff and the rope. He began leading the cow with the rope, walking away from Paradise, up the hill from whence he had come.

The Trip

A whisper of air that passes through the reeds makes them sway and, as they bend with the wind, one can see a boat moored in a small cove. From the bow, the profile of an old Hatteras sports fisherman arches softly to the brow, and gracefully continues to reach beyond the rear of the cabin at the level of the rails of the fishing platform at the stern. That and the many angles of the lines comprising the cabin and the fly bridge may be what make her so elegant. She seems restless but staid. She seems patient but eager to get under way. Or it may be that she awakens in so many a yearn to go back to the sea. She entices them to the idea of being part of that journey that brings them closer to where they should be: the sea; to the sea that beacons men and women to return to where they must have begun so many years ago. That they can't is irrelevant. Don't you see? It is the idea of it—not a realistic notion of what can be. And so, sailors and want-to-be-sailors do go back to the sea. Some never return. Somehow, she knows, and still readies to take them into that journey.

A soft light breaks the night mantle showing the silent deck. By the left rail, away from the shore, a silent man stoops hanging on to the stainless-steel pipe. Gray hair covers his head. One could say that he is frail, but the arms and shoulders visible out of his sleeveless t-shirt show sinewy muscles as if he worked them hard. It is a cool September night in the south coast of Key Largo. The light of the full moon hides many stars, and there is a rumor of waves slapping the keel.

As Jorge leans on the rail, he wonders what they could have done different. Was there anything that could give them a better chance? What they plan has so very little chance of success. As he looks into the dark of the night, he hears soft paces approaching.

From below deck, a woman appears. She is aged, but in a graceful way. Her mid-length hair is still red but without the glow and sheen of her youth. She is still pretty with distracting green eyes. Clad in a black tee-shirt and jeans, there is an air of youth about her. She is a short woman who appears taller than she is, except when she stands next to her obviously tall husband John. Her slender figure moves without effort appearing to glide more than to walk.

He turns to her and asks with hesitation clearly in his voice,

- Are you sure you want to go through with this, Elizabeth? We can still cancel this trip. Look, it's an old boat, and ...

- We've been through all this." Elizabeth cuts in. "Let it go, Jorge. We're going.

- All right, Liz. I'll pull the anchor and start the engines. Loosen the lines and we'll be under way.

She knows that he calls her Liz when he is unhappy with her because he knows she does not like it, but she decides to ignore it and goes about untying the lines from the mooring. In a moment she can hear the engines running and feels the boat start to move away from the land into the depth of the night.

He holds on the wheel staring at the empty darkness very aware of her presence next to him.

- How long? she asks.

- You know I don't know. I'm no sailor, but we're probably about 30 miles from Key West. Habana is a bit more than a hundred miles from there. If this speedometer thing is any clue, we're doing about 10 MPH. I don't know how that translates to nautical miles. Don't ask. I don't know how to calculate for drift due to currents either. The only things that give us a chance are the electronics: the GPS and the automatic pilot. I guess that if we can keep this speed, we can expect contact between 10 and 13 hours. But I'm just guessing. How are you doing down there, John?

- I'm fine. Don't worry about me.

John is a third-generation immigrant. His Russian and Polish ancestors were of modest means while his English and Greek heritage is aristocratic. Only his white beard and moustache hint at his true age, but looking closely one can see that his black hair is faded, thinning on top. He moves with unusual grace, perhaps from his years as a gymnast in his youth. Although he is a well-respected professional musician and academician, he has a love of guns, and he's very good using them. He tends to be a kind and easy-going man, but one would not want to cross him.

- We have fuel for 50 hours. If I stray off course for any length of time, we could be toast.

- Then don't stray, man -, offers John.

- Right. Did you check the guns?

- We practiced shooting the guns and the machine gun, we practiced going to different places using the boat electronics, we installed that stupid bullet proof door and my closet with its camera and sound system, we have done all we could. We have a good plan. Try to relax. Do you want me to take the wheel?

- No. We can't risk on anyone seeing you. Sit tight. I will be all right in a minute.

Elizabeth, no longer able to keep silence, says emphatically **-,** This was your idea; your plan. Get it together. Now.

- You're right," Jorge says taking a deep breath. "Let's do this." "One final check: satellite phone?

Elizabeth checks and replies,

- Working.

- Flares?

- Check -, John replies.

- Marine radio?

- Check -, Elizabeth replies.

- Fishing rods?"- Check, check, check. We have the bait, the fishing licenses, the Mexican flag, the boat registration, all the god-damn things you forced us to buy, and we know what each of us needs to do. I need a drink and a smoke -, says Elizabeth.

John says from below,

- No, you don't. Just breathe.

- We'll be ok. An old couple out on fishing trip that gets lost a bit due to lack of experience. And if the Coast guard stops us: three people fishing. Lights are good. Registration is good. Engines are good. Boat is solid. The mods are great. We're good to go -, says Jorge.

With silence in the boat, only the purring of the 500HP engines break the silence of the night as the 45 ft Hatteras sport fisherman hugs the coast cruising south to Key West. No one speaks.

- It is a crazy idea -, Jorge was thinking -, but it's her only chance. We're the only ones that are willing to go this far. If we all die? So what? We've been there. Done that. Done what? Whatever. Probably hundreds of damn holes lurk in this plan. I don't know where they get their strength. Damn heroes! Not me. Rely on the electronics? Sure. What about what they say about electronics going crazy in the Bahamas' triangle. I didn't tell them. Maybe they know. We sure are going in there. Hey, but millions of people go boating, cruising and fishing there. What's one more trip without incidence? Are you listening, universe? - Silence.

Jorge picks-up the satellite phone and dials.

- Yeah? - a voice at the other end asks.

- We're off towards Cuba. Turn on the clock.

- Right. Good luck!

- You too -, he says hanging up. – Well -, he thinks -, that's that.

Jorge's background of relative poverty contrasting with being a member of a family of renown, mixed with his higher education and cultural experiences made him a strange person. Perhaps that is why he was so close to Elizabeth. She with a background of poor North Carolinian factory workers on her father's side and an aristocratic family on her mother's side that dated back to the 17th century. That her mother's ancestors once owned nearly 300 hundred slaves still troubled her. Odd people. Maybe they were close because both lost their fathers at a very early age. In any case, they were very good friends. Like her father would have been, Jorge was very proud to be her friend. In spite of everything life threw at her, here she was: a doctor of letters.

To his right, he sees the lights of a city. "Key West," he thinks. Looking at the instruments, he verifies that it is time to veer left towards Habana. He types-in the new coordinates, and thinks, "Well that's that.

I'll ask Elizabeth to take the wheel. We should be all right for a few hours. I hope I can sleep a couple of hours."

- With one last look around, he steps down the stairs past the galley, to the main berth -, Elizabeth? -, he calls softly as he nudges her shoulder.

- What is it? Have they called?

- No. Do you think you can take over so that I can try to sleep a bit?

- Sure. Give me a minute to get some coffee and I will come up. John?

- Asleep. I don't know how he does it.

- Yes. He's a rock.

With Elizabeth at the wheel, John sleeping soundly, and Jorge tossing and turning restlessly, four hours passed. "I guess we're on a fool's errant," Elizabeth thought. "Maybe. But if there's a chance, we've got to take the risk, and John's right. We have done all we could do. Desperate people on a desperate journey facing desperate odds. I could use a tequila, or four, and a smoke. Right now! Jorge is a little bit shaky, but John is steady. I wonder if John really realizes the danger, we're in? We should have brought the dogs. Who's going to take care of them if we don't make it? I could use the company of one of those bullies. Dogs relax me. Look at that brilliant moon! Look at the sea! So peaceful now; how can it be so frightfully dreadful sometimes? It does not seem possible."

The sound of the satellite phone startles her. She calls down loudly:

- Jorge. It's the phone.

Elizabeth hears a sharp voice at the other end say,

- Write this down. Are you ready?

Grabbing a pencil and the note pad, Elizabeth nervously says -, Yes.

- 24.637773 North, 81.826553 West. I will call back in twenty minutes. You will tell me then your expected time of arrival. Be ready. - The voice on the other end sounds steady and resolute.

The line goes dead. Jorge comes up the stairs a bit groggy. John is listening at the bottom of the stairs. Sharp.

- Here are the coordinates -, Elizabeth shows Jorge. - We need to calculate our time of arrival. They will call back in twenty minutes. - She stares at him, her eyes reflecting both fear and determination.

- OK. We're on. You want to do it, or do you want me to?

- I'll do it -, Elizabeth says this time with firmness in her voice.

She punches-in the coordinates and redirects the auto pilot. Out comes the news.

- We will be there in about one hour, forty-seven minutes at this rate of speed -, Elizabeth tells them.

- OK. John, it's time to load the guns and get ready. I am going to get some coffee. Anyone else?

- Yes -, says Elizabeth.

- Me too -, says John.

So, they drink their coffee, John at the galley, Jorge and Elizabeth at the helm.

John casts glances at the pair of friends above the stairs wondering what would make Jorge go this far. He and Elizabeth, he knew. They really had to. But Jorge, he could not understand. Friendship can only go so far. It's not as if he doesn't realize the bind, we're in. He's obviously really concerned. I don't know if afraid is the word. He is hanging in there. What drives the man?

The sound of the phone again.

- Hello -, Elizabeth says, this time calmly.

- When will you arrive?

- In about one hour and thirty minutes.

- OK. We will call you again then.

As the line goes dead, they glance at each other silently. What more could be said? Time seemed to go faster. One hour.

Jorge feels the wind picking up. He knows what to do. He calls down to John.

- OK, John. It's time. Do what you have to get ready to go into your hole. Let me know if you can hear us and see us.

- Check.

A few minutes later, John says,

- I'm in. I can see you. Speak.

- OK. Are you going to be all right in there?

- I will be fine.

- Love you, John.

- I love you too, Elizabeth.

- All right. Fifteen minutes then -, Jorge reminds them.

- Jorge -, Elizabeth says -, no matter what happens, you are a dear friend, and I love you.

- Thanks. I love you too. Now, let's see if love can help us.

- Any time, John. Please maintain silence -, Jorge says.

- OK.

The phone rings. Elizabeth picks it up.

- Yes?

- Turn your running light off and on three times.

- OK -, she says and turns the switch as the man asked her.

- If you want your daughter alive, you will do exactly as I say. - Have the data disc ready for us. We're coming aboard. - The voice sounds demanding.

Off to the right, the sound of another boat announces its presence. Elizabeth places the engines on idle and turns to her right to wait for the borders. Jorge places a set of bumpers on the right side of the boat and steps back. Soon, two men climb over the rail and tie a line to the Hatteras. Both dressed in black, they appear forceful and threatening.

- Where is the disc? Give it to me -, a muscular man says with a large hand gun pointed at them.

- You will get it when you give us my daughter -, Elizabeth demanded.

- We're not fooling with you. Give me the disc or I'll start shooting now!

- If you fire, no matter what, you will not get the disc. Come on, we're here, there's nowhere for us to go, we've done all you asked, give us something. You're going to get your disc. Where is Michelle? -, says Jorge in a steady voice.

- Get over here you two. On your knees, you son-of-a-bitch.

- You too, bitch.

As Jorge and Elizabeth kneel, the men come behind them and place guns to the back of their heads.

- Now, we're going to start shooting if we don't get the disc. Where is it?

Behind them, John closes the bullet-prove glass door and calmly says,

- I have it."

The two men turn hurriedly around keeping Elizabeth and Jorge in front of them.

- Who in the hell are you?

- I am the man that will only be paid if the girl returns to the US with me. So, where is she?

- Fuck you. What we need here is the disc. If we don't get it, we will start shooting these people. - Only one man spoke. The other remained silent.

- If you kill them, you kill them. I only care about the girl. Hell, if you don't kill them, I will. My bullets will rip right through them and tear you apart. Do you know what a hollow-point magnum does in this distance? I'm done talking. Where is the girl?

- Hey, take it easy, guy -, Jorge says wondering where in the hell the 45-magnum came from -, nobody has to die here. Just give him the girl, we will give you the disc, and everybody wins. Otherwise, there will be a lot of blood for nothing. Common, everybody be cool.

The two borders stare menacingly at John, then at each other, and the silent smaller man says. - She's in the boat. Give us the disc, and you can have her.

- That's reasonable -, Jorge agreed.

- No -, Elizabeth breaks in -, bring the girl aboard, and we will give you the disc.

- OK. Keep the gun on this one, the silent guy who was no longer silent told the other guy. I'll go for the girl. If anybody moves, shoot her -, he orders pointing at Elizabeth.

An uneasy silence keeps everyone waiting nervously.

- Here she is, and she is going to be dead if I don't get the disc right now.

Things people plan, hardly ever come out exactly as they expect them. There was one guy behind Michelle, the other behind Elizabeth, Jorge kneeling to one side, and John aiming his gun trying to find a target.

Jorge dives to the ground. The gunman on Elizabeth and the one on Michelle turn their guns to him, and there is the sound of two shots. The two men collapse. Shot in the head. Impossible odds, but there it was, the crazy people are still alive.

Jorge grabs one of the men's guns and turns to the other boat. Elizabeth grabs Michelle's arm and drags her, John opens the door, and the two women race below deck.

A light onto the other boat does not show any movement. Jorge climbs the side and searches the boat.

- Hey, John. There is another girl tied-up below deck.

- Bring her up and let's get out of here.

A slim young woman with blond hair blowing over her face appears and stumbles as she moves beside Jorge.

- Right. Turn off all lights, John. Here we go -, he says as he guides the other girl onto the boat and urges her to go below deck. Her feet are unsteady and her eyes show confusion and relief.

With coordinates to Key West in the auto-pilot, Jorge pushes the gear as far as it can go. The big diesels roar and as the boat picks-up speed, it rises from the sea and seems to fly away close to the calm ocean through now gentle breezes.

- Call the Coast Guard, Elizabeth -, John calls down to Elizabeth urgently.

- Right -, she responds coming up to check the instruments.

- United States Coast Guard.

- This is the Speedy Maiden out of Key West. We're at the

following coordinates 24.102889 North 81.783389 West on the way to Key West cruising at 45 Knots with running lights off. We have just been attacked at sea. We don't know if we're being followed. Please let us know where you can meet us. We may be in need of medical assistance.

- Stand by.

- Do we throw these men overboard? -, asks John.

- I don't know. We can't get rid of the blood. What do you think, Elizabeth?

- I say we keep them. The law might know who they are. I don't think getting rid of the bodies will help us. There's blood all over the deck, and that girl below. How do we explain those things to the Coast Guard?

- Continue your course and speed. The USCGC Hamilton will meet you in three hours. She bears the ID number 715. You must turn-on your running lights in no more than two hours.

- Yes. Thank you. Thank you -, responds Elizabeth. - I'm going down to check on the girls -, she remarks, and goes below deck.

- Good shooting, John. I know I couldn't have done it. Amazing, really -, Jorge remarks.

- Yes. It is a hard thing to kill people, but those two guys sure made it a bit easier. How's it going down there, Elizabeth?

- Michelle's trying to get it together. The other girl is confused. She's crying. I can't seem to do anything for her.

- Hug her -, John offers.

- Damn, looks like we have company -, Jorge says pointing at the running lights to the rear of the boat. - What the hell is that? It is keeping up with us. They're moving fast and must have radar to see us in the dark. What do you think, John? -, Jorge asks urgently.

- We can't go any faster. If they can't either, we should be ok, but I'll get on the machine gun just in case.

Just as he finishes speaking, the sound of a machine gun blasts the silence of the night. Tracer bullets arch in the direction of the fisherman. John races up the stairs to the fly bridge, raises the heavy canvas, and uncovers the machine gun. He turns towards the following craft, puts-on his ear muffs, aims the machine gun, and pulls the trigger. The first tracer bullets are short. It was hard to say by how much. The other tracer bullets were coming much closer. John adjusts the machine gun again and shoots continuously for several seconds. A flash of light rises from sea with the roar of an explosion where the following boat now blazes in flames in the night air.

John comes down from the fly bridge staggering. There is blood in his right arm. As he approaches Jorge, he notices that he is also bleeding.

Alarmed, he asks -, Where did you get it, Jorge?

- My left side. I think it will be okay if we can stop the bleeding. Your arm? - Jorge asks with obvious pain in his voice.

- Just a scratch. Let's see what Elizabeth can do. How far are we from the rendezvous?

- I'd say two hours. A man could die in two hours.

- Cry baby! Let's go.

With John holding on to one side of the hand rail and Jorge the other they make it down the stairs. Elizabeth, who does not notice the blood, asks,

- Both of you here? Who's at the helm?

- It was on auto-pilot -, Jorge says.

- We'll be back up in a while. Who's good with bandages? -, John asks.

- What?! -, Elizabeth exclaims as she notices the blood stains on their clothes and moves quickly towards them.

- Don't make a big deal of this. We are both OK. We just need to stop the bleeding -, John says.

- I can do it -, a weak voice came from the other side of the room -, I am a doctor.

- That is good to hear, but so young and a doctor already? What's your name? -, asks Jorge.

- I'm Kelly. Do we have a First Aid Kit? -, she says ignoring Jorge's remark.

- We have tons -, says John. - We kind of felt something like this might happen. Here it is -, he says pulling a suitcase from a closet.

- Can you take the helm for a little while, Elizabeth? This shouldn't take long.

- For as long as it takes. Don't let them make you hurry, Kelly.

- I'm coming with you, mom.

Kelly works fast. She takes a look at the wounds, gives Jorge a towel and asks him to press it against his side. In a moment she cleans John's arm and bandages it. Then it's Jorge's turn. After she cleans the wound, she takes a couple of stitches and bandages the wound.

- Come on, cry baby, let's see what's on top?

- Yes, yes, Superman, just give me a minute. I'll be up there.

- Thanks, Kelly. How much of a mechanic are you?

- Not that.

- Sorry. There's no time for being nice. We're not home yet. I need to check the engines below, and I might need help coming up the stairs.

- I see. Show the way.

On the way down from the upper deck Jorge noticed a few bullets holes on the upper and lower decks. It was fortunate that they missed the women but he wanted to see if they had damaged anything below. He looks around as if he knew what he was doing. All he could really tell was that there was no smoke and the engines sounded normal. The light is on and there is no fire. So, he climbs up the stairs, passes by Kelly at the top, and heads for the main deck. Half way, he turns to Kelly and says,

- Hey, there are sandwiches and sodas in the fridge if you're hungry. Maybe a beer?

- I already had a drink and I can't eat right now. I'll go up with you.

They find Elizabeth and John wondering what to do. A bullet hit the instruments and the lights are dead.

- How about the GPS in the phone? -, John asks. - Never mind, no roads here.

- Not a bad idea. It at least shows the direction of travel. Do we have a compass? -, asks Jorge. - With all the electronics in the boat, I guess nobody thought to bring a compass.

- My iPhone has an app for that, but how do we use it? -, says Elizabeth.

- We can try to maintain a North by Northeast direction and hope we hit Florida somewhere. If we miss the boot, we may hit the panhandle if we're lucky and have enough fuel. We'd never make it to Mexico. Otherwise, we can go straight north for five or six hours, and then go west until we hit land. In either case, we would just be guessing our way.

- Hold on, Jorge. I'll call the Coast Guard. They will think of something -, says Elizabeth. - Where is the satellite phone?

They all looked around in search of the phone that nobody could find as the boat miraculously maintained a straight course to an unknown destination.

- Wait a moment, Jorge, didn't you make Bill and Craig buy a bunch of back-up electronics?

- You're right, John. Where are they? Elizabeth was supposed to learn how to use that stuff?

- Don't look at me. You're the damn engineer.

- Who doesn't know how to use them because he hasn't read the user manuals.

- It can't be that hard. Let's look through the stuff and see what we find -, offers John.

- Wait, what about the steering? -, asks Elizabeth.

- The boat does not seem to have taken a sharp turn. Let's pray that it is still on our heading and stays on it until we can figure out how to use the spare GPS. Pull out your iPhone and find our current direction of travel. Try to keep the boat steady in that same direction.

- OK.

- I'll help mom.

- I'll stay too. Don't move too fast you two and start bleeding again.

- Yes, mother. Find the satellite phone. I have to call Bill. -, Jorge says moving gingerly down the stairs.

- Hold on tight -, says John as he follows Jorge down the steps in search of the spare electronics.

....

About a week earlier, a slender ordinary man sits alertly listening to a bespectacled, heavy man clad with a white coat.

- Fred, you asked me to tell you the truth, so I will do that. I'm afraid that your heart is not going to make it another month. There's not going to be a transplant either. With your emphysema, you probably wouldn't survive the operation even if we could get this approved.

- What if I paid for the operation?

- You would need a heart, and the donor program would not approve the transplant.

- Another country with fewer restrictions?

- There is that, but you must know that your chances are very limited in any case.

- Thank you, doctor -, says the man getting up and offering his hand.

- Good luck, Fred.

- Yeah.

"Well," the man thinks stepping on the elevator on his way out, "in a way, it removes all restrictions on what I can do. What can anyone do to a dead man? And if I have any kind of a chance, I should take it. Sure, it takes money, but I know where there is plenty of that. Those overseas accounts, I can create new ones and transfer the money. And if I'm going to do one, I might as well do all of them. There must be nearly 500 hundred million dollars in those accounts. I can get a new heart and change my face. If I come out of this, I will be set for life. If not, I was going to die anyway. I'm going to need some help. Who can I trust? The attorney. He seems to be a good man. Married, with that kid. I wonder if I offered him a million if he would help me. First things first. The accounts.

I'm sure that when they find out, they're going to come looking for blood, but a dead man cannot care what happens to his blood."

He calls a cab and goes home. Pulls out his computer and starts typing. A while later, he gets on the phone.

- This is Fred Carter. I wonder if I can come over to see you in a few minutes?

- Fred, I am in the middle of something. I'll be busy all afternoon, and I promised that I would take Michelle and her parents out to dinner later.

- It is extremely important for both of us, and it will only take fifteen minutes of your time.

- OK. We're going to Puckett's restaurant on 5th and Church. My family will arrive at 7. I can meet you there at 6:30. Does that work for you?

- It will have to.

But nobody leaves hundreds of millions of dollars in the care of just one person. The backup guy, checking on the deposits, finds to his amazement that there's no money in the accounts. He calls his supervisor who calls Fred who does not answer because he knows that the rabbit is out of the hat.

Thinking frantically, he knows that they will come looking for him. He records the account numbers and passwords onto a disc, places the disc on a plastic holder, writes a note, places everything on a manila folder and writes the name of the attorney on the envelope. He goes out to find a cab, drives to the attorney's office and drops the envelope at the desk. It probably wasn't going to happen anyway, so fuck them. The Group V people lose the money anyway. He pads the gun on his side pocket and calmly walks down the street to a bar where he knows they'll find him. He sits facing the entrance door, orders a drink, and begins sipping his drink in the nearly empty bar.

After a while, two men enter the bar, he recognizes them, he gets up for the stool, pulls his gun out of his pocket and advances towards them carefully aiming the gun with two hands. He was thinking, "Dead men don't talk."

The two men go for their guns, and the sounds of shots fill the bar. There is Fred, dead on the floor. One of the two men is also dead. The other one searches Fred and finds nothing. He takes Fred's cell phone and leaves the bar reeling from his side wound. When the man reports what happened in the bar, the search for the money begins.

The Group V organization was created by Victor Grossen. Of teutonic descend, he grew-up in the Stuyvesant Square neighborhood of New York city of the 40's. It was a place where Italians predominated. Being of German origin during the second world war in this neighborhood was not an easy thing to do. Blonde hair and blue eyes made him stand out. One either turned steel tough, or one shriveled away. Victor turned steel tough. He was a boy with a husky voice who learned how to fight out of necesity and lost in those fights any sense of sensibility.

In his fifties, he moved to Nashville, TN. He sought a place that would afford him low visibility while giving him a change of scenery. He thought that the south might be more welcoming to him, and Nashville seemed to be ideal.

There, he decided to create an organization that took advantage of the existing demands for solutions to the nagging prison issues of the times, the horrific demand for young children slaves and prostitutes, and the growing demand for human organs. To take advantage of these situations, he partnered with a Caribbean sea dictator to create what he called a "human processing plant." There, he instructed the plant manager to segregate young attrative people so that they could be sold abroad as slaves and/or prostitutes. The next group was composed of healthy but not quite attrative people. Those he ordered designated for human-organ harvesting. Finally, he ordered that those who did not fit in either category, be killed and cremated. He ordered the creation of an industrial diamond factory using those ashes.

His spiel to government agencies and country strong-men was simple:

"Hard times demand tough decisions. Your prisons and your mental hospitals are crowded. It costs too much money to maintain these institutions. Your street people scare away turism. I can help. On a one-time cost basis, you gather up these people and send them to my base. After that, they're my problem. You never have to see them or spend money on them again."

His plant soon ran to capacity, and he had to increase capacity to handle the demand. Money came in at such a fast rate that he had to create unusual ways of managing it. Off shore accounts helped a bit, but he also created money-storage safe locations to have quick access to the funds. To handle increased capacity, he also created a support organization comprised of other insensitive, money hungry people. Whether one might believe this man to be insane or not is somewhat questionable, but one would surely believe that this man was extremely dangerous.

When Victor learned that his offshore accounts were empty, his steely cold eyes looked furiously at the man reporting the news.

- Where is Fred? -, he demanded.

- Dead. I sent Josh and Mick to find him. They shot it out with him. Josh got it, Mick got a bullet on his side. He told me what happened.

- And did you tell those idiots that we needed Fred alive to find out what happened to the money?

- Yes, I did. But Mick says that Fred came out shooting and there was nothing they could do to bring him back alive.

- Well, you send Tom to finish Mick. I'll be damn if he gets away with thinking that his life is more important than my money. And find everything there is to know about Fred. I want to know everything: everything he did today, who his relatives are, who his friends are, who his associates are, I want to know everything. Is that clear?

- Yes, sir. I'll get right on it.

As oftentimes happens, very important things receive little or no attention. The secretary hands the attorney the manila envelope on his way out. He takes it without glancing at it and goes to the car, already late for his diner appointment and having forgotten about Fred altogether. He tosses the folder on the passenger seat and drives to the restaurant where he picks up the envelope not knowing why and places it in his right coat pocket, not on the left where he had the papers he had promised to take to Elizabeth.

During diner, he gives Elizabeth the wrong envelope. She pays no attention to the folded envelope, putting it away in her purse.

Days later, when in the search of the money, Fred's taxi ride to the attorney's office is uncovered together with the call he made on his cell phone, visitors come to ask the attorney some hard questions for which he has no answers, so they kidnap his wife Michelle to convince him that they are serious people.

At about that time, Elizabeth finally gets around to opening the manila envelope and reads Fred's note.

> This disc contains offshore accounts of the Group V organization. They are very evil people. The total amount of funds in these accounts is about 500 million dollars. I will probably be dead when you read this. It is extremely important that you do not do anything to let these people know that you have this information. They will surely do anything to recover this money, and they will kill you even if you return it to them, so make sure nobody finds out that it exists.

It's hard to say why Elizabeth calls Jorge at a time like this. Perhaps it is a desire to release tension in some way, but she knows that she could tell him anything, so she tells him everything.

- Wow. What do you want to do about this?

- I don't know. I've never been in a situation like this.

- Most people haven't, but this needs action. Do you want my help?

- What in the world could you do?

- I don't know. Perhaps just to add another point of view to a discussion between you, John, and your son-in-law because that has to happen. I don't want to butt-in, but I am available if you want me to come over.

- Have you thought that getting involved in this could get you killed?

- Yes. I kind of figured that out, but what the hell, I'll be dead soon enough without this. As an outsider I would be a bit less affected by some outcomes, and that might give you another perspective. It's up to you.

- Oh, hell. Just come on down, but hurry. The Group V people are not fooling around.

- I'll try to be there tomorrow. In the meantime, you may want to see if you can access those accounts. Whatever you do, you'll need plenty of cash.

- Right.

And Elizabeth checks and finds out that she can access the accounts, but getting the money is something else. Most of the money is in the Grand Cayman Island. She calls Jorge back to let him know.

- Why don't you, John and I meet at the Grand Cayman Island instead of Tennessee? Those people will soon have you located in Nashville and then it will be hard to come out of this well.

- What do we do there?

- Plan a course of action where we can have access to the funds needed to implement it. Ask John what he thinks.

- He's listening in. John?

- Aside from going to the police with this, I have no idea, but that would place Michelle's life in greater danger.

- Listen -, says Jorge -, I'm going to say something very harsh, but I think it's important. Whatever you decide to do, it would relieve your stress considerably if you start with the notion that this mess is going to get everyone killed. So don't worry about it. We probably can't do anything about it. But of course, we need to try.

- That's an awful thing to say -, says Elizabeth.

- Yes, it is. Well? Elizabeth?

- OK.

- John?

- Damn! OK.

- Ok. They don't know me but they're probable closing in on you. Get rid of the cell phones. Get a wad of cash and stop using the credit cards. Call me when you get to Grand Cayman. Good luck. I'm off to find tickets -, Jorge says as he hangs up.

- John, these people are not ever going to let us in peace. We need to do something about them.

- What do you mean?

- I believe that it's them or us, and I definitely want it to be them.

- What can we do?

- Not us. We need to find some people that can take care of it.

- What kind of people?

- Professionals.

- Like who?

- I used to know a guy. I think I still have his phone somewhere. With all this money, we can hire an army to take care of these people if we just had enough time.

- This is getting crazier every minute, but what the hell. If Jorge is right, unless we do some crazy things, we're not surviving this. Call the guy. I'll check the airlines.

- Right.

Why people hang on to some past history is hard to say. But Elizabeth called the old number and managed to find the guy.

- Hi, Bill. I am glad I found you. This is Elizabeth.

- What the hell, Liz, where did you come from? How are you doing? -, he says recognizing her voice.

- I don't have time to be nice. I need your help. Can you meet me in Grand Cayman Island tomorrow so that we can discuss this? If you can't make it, I need you to send someone who can be there and does the type of things you used to do. You will need a team to take care of this. I am in a position to pay for this. Do you understand?

- I happen to have the time. How do I contact you when I arrive?

- Call 555-730-1237. Jorge, a friend of mine, will know how to get in touch. Thank you, Bill. I have to run now. Bye.

- John?

- Got the tickets. Tomorrow at ten.

- OK. I found my guy. He will meet us in Grand Cayman. Let's pack light, leave the house, and stay at an airport hotel until we leave. I called Carmina. We can leave the dogs with her. I don't like the idea of staying here any longer.

- Makes sense. Let's do it.

Crazy situations make people crazy, and they do crazy things that somehow make sense.

If you are going to die in the near future, you might as well enjoy your last days. So, Jorge (because he thinks he can still use his credit cards without leaving a trail) makes reservations for everyone at the Ritz

Carlton—one of the best hotels in the island. That sets up the first meeting between Bill, Elizabeth, John and Jorge. John is a bit uneasy about the association with Bill and to avoid that Elizabeth asks Jorge to handle the meeting with Bill and leave them out of it.

Bill is around forty years old, about six-feet tall, muscular, with dark hair and eyes, and a calm demeanor that does not hint at the way he makes a living. His easy smile is disarming.

Jorge explains to Bill what happened in the last few days. Mulling this over, Bill asks -, What are we talking about in this situation, Jorge?

- The Group V people told the attorney that they're going to kill anyone that opposes their recovery of their money. Fred, the guy that gave us the disc, told us in a note that they'll also kill anyone who knows about the money even if they recover it. That means that we have a situation where the only safe thing to do for Elizabeth and her family is to eradicate anyone associated with these people—from their soldiers to the heads of the organization. John was worried that if he or Elizabeth were to ask you to take care of this, there would be legal implications for them. I see that danger, but for me, there is no other recourse for their future safety.

- How many people are we talking about?

- I don't really know, but I suspect that it's about 20 to 30 people.

- To be clear, are you asking me to create a team of paramilitary people for the purpose of killing all these people?

- Yes, I am. And in the process, I want you to have these four priorities:

- Do research to identify targets making sure that you find all of them.

- Kill them all.

- Do so in the safest way for you and your people.

- If you can do it without risking your life and that of your people, do an asset recovery. There is bound to be a lot of cash around in the environment of these people.

- Are you willing to take this on?"

- I'm going to need a large group of people to take this on.

- I imagine that at least 50 people.

- That is going to cost a lot of money.

- What do you estimate the cost?

- If I go with fifty people, at about $50,000 per person, that is $2.5 Million plus expenses, but I won't know how many people I will need until I do the research.

- Let's estimate $6 Million, We give you $3 Million now, and you get the rest when the job is done. That is what you need to tell your people. Because we don't know if we'll come out of this alive, we'll open an account for you here and deposit the other 3 million to ensure that you'll be paid whether we survive or not. Does that cover the cost of the operation?

- Damn. You don't fool around, do you?

- There is no time. We're going to need a fast boat that does not call attention to itself or to us. I know. Fast boats call attention to themselves.

- You know, I have a friend that has a 1985, 45 ft. Hatteras Sport

Fisherman. Nobody's going to believe that this old boat is fast, but he installed three gas turbines combined with surface drives generating 13,620hp driving three waterjets for a maximum speed of 50 knots. She also has two conventional engines with twin screws for easier maneuverability at low speed. He also has all the electronics needed for the boat to practically sail itself. You just have to provide the coordinates of your destination and the electronics do the rest.

- How do we get this boat?

- It's moored about thirty miles north of Key West. If you want this boat, you need to give this guy $8 Million. That is what he is asking for the boat.

- That's fine. I also want to install one heavy turret machine gun on the fly bridge of the fisherman in a way that we can fire it in any direction. And we'll need instructions for this thing. Can you help me with that?

- I don't know if I can get you the latest thing, but I can get something that's near that. And yes, I can have it installed. We'll have to remove the anything on the fly bridge to allow the machine gun to fire in any direction, but we can do that.

- Great, we will also need some precision 9mm handguns. Three should do it. Of course, plenty of ammo for everything. And we'll need a back-up for every major electronic component of that boat. These back-ups need to be something we can set up in the event that the existing units are damaged. I would prefer handheld devices but if that is not doable, I want something that we can carry without breaking our backs. Your friend should know what to get. You and him will provide a list of these items with the instructions. And finally, we will need a heavy-duty satellite telephone. Have you got all that?

- Yes. I have a great memory, and I see what you are after. Do you need a crew?

- I have not discussed any of this with the others. I need to get their approval before we go forward, but I don't think we want to put anyone in a dangerous situation, or depend on people that don't have the same commitment that we have on this situation. I will get back to you on that. You will have the final go in a few hours. In the meantime, ask your friend to hold on to the boat until he hears from you.

- OK.

As Jorge walks away to meet with Elizabeth and John, he is a bit giddy. In a way what he is going to ask them to do is so preposterous that there is little chance that they would approve the plan. On the other hand, if they did approve his plan, the GV people were sure to buy into it because it seemed to place them in complete control. And they would probably be right, except that desperate people can sometimes overcome terrible odds, and that self-confidence might be the undoing of the GV people.

Jorge calls ahead to let them know he is coming. John lets him in the room.

- What now, Jorge?

- I gave Bill some instructions but asked him to wait until I discuss it with you to find out if you approve everything. I'm not going to discuss what I asked Bill to do about these people. The only thing you need to know is that I promised to give him $6 Million dollars tomorrow. The other thing is a crazy proposal I came up with on what to do next. Have you thought of anything about that?

- What do you mean? -, says Elizabeth.

- Here's the situation as I see it. These people are holding

Michelle. We don't know if she's still alive. All we know is that they want their money back at any cost, and that they intend to kill us all. Does that cover it? -, asks Jorge.

- I wish you were not so damn cavalier about the life of my daughter!

- Sorry. We need to look at the reality of this situation as clearly as possible.

- Well, let's agree that is reality. What can we do? -, asks John.

- Elizabeth, do you have any ideas?

- All I know is what we cannot do. We can't give them back the money. It wouldn't do any good. We can't reason with this people. We need a plan to recover Michelle without doing those things.

- Ok. John, I seem to recall that Elizabeth said that you were a great shot with just about anything that one can use. Is that correct?

- I guess.

- Elizabeth, you can also shoot well as I recall.

- Not nearly as good as John.

- I can shoot a little too.

- I remember -, Elizabeth says.

- Here is my plan. We contact those people and tell them that we can give them a disc with the account numbers and passwords so that they can recover their money in exchange for Michelle. We'll also say that to do this in a way that is safe for everyone, we will meet them in the high seas between Key West and Cuba. Doing this in international waters will avoid interference from any government entity. Also, doing this will make the GV people believe that they can prepare themselves to take the disc and kill us all in one single action—which might in fact happen; however, if we're lucky, they will show us Michelle thinking that they are in control, and that we don't have the ability to face up to them. If that happens, and they bring Michelle to our boat, John may be able to shoot whoever shows up for them to our boat. It is a long shot, but that is all I have. What do you think?"

- You are right -, says John -, it's a crazy idea. How many more ifs could a plan have? Who's going to be captain to steer the boat, where is this boat coming from, what are we using for guns, what makes you think they will not shoot first and ask questions later?

- And what guarantees do we have that they will even bring Michelle to the boat? -, adds Elizabeth.

- Some of those questions are on the money, and there are no good answers for them. On the other hand, we can get guns and a great boat through Bill. The boat has modern electronics that would allow any of us to go from point A to point B given the coordinates. I doubt if these guys will start shooting before they get their hands on the disc, and I know that very few people shoot as well as John.

- Say that works -, says Elizabeth -, what stops them from having multiple boats—and very fast boats as smugglers have, equipped with heavy weapons, how do we get away?

- Good questions. The boat I have in mind has been modified. It runs a maximum of 50 knots. There are not too many boats that can move that fast in heavy seas.

- What about one of those, what do they call them? Cigarrettes? -, asks John.

- Yes. There is that, John. I don't know how fast they can go or for how long. This is something we may have to look into. But our boat will also have a heavy turret machine gun on a tripod in the fly bridge that will be able to fire in any direction. Can you fire one of those, John?

- I have fired a heavy machine gun. Where are you getting that?

- Bill.

- How do we contact the GV people without giving them our location? -, asks Elizabeth. - Once they locate us, we will have little options.

- We can send them instructions through a FAX just before we leave Grand Cayman. I asked Bill to get a satellite phone for us. I don't know that they will be able to track that, but we will use it only when we are under way towards international waters.

- Not from Grand Cayman -, says Elizabeth. - We arrange for a FedEx store in somewhere like Michigan to receive the FAX and forward it to them. That will slow them down a bit, but really, what are our chances in all this? -, asks Elizabeth.

- A little bit better than when we started -, says John -, but just a little.

- This is just a suggestion. I am open to whatever you come up with -, says Jorge.

- I think that anything we come up with will be just as hard to do -, says Elizabeth -, and we don't have a lot of time to dwell on what to do. If you are game, John, I am willing.

- They can't kill dead people -, John says. - Let's go for it!

- Ok. Tomorrow, we need to give Bill six million for his part and find out how we pay eight million for the boat. Don't you like the way we can throw millions at the wind?

- Let's pray they do some good -, says Elizabeth.

- Amen -, says John.

Jorge walks off picking-up his cell to call Bill.

- Hello.

- Let's get a drink downstairs at the Jack Bar.

- Be right down.

Down the hall to the elevator, Jorge was thinking, "Normally, few things happen in a few hours. This is not normal, so much to crunch in so little time, so much that we can miss, I wish there was insurance for this, some form of back-up... I guess you could want all you want, but it is what it is."

He walks out of the lobby, into the dusk and by the pool to the bar. A truly wild sunset embraces the horizon in the distance. Jorge barely notices its startling beauty as he walks to the table where Bill already has a drink.

- Bill.

- Yeah.

- We're on. A few questions. How long will it take you to set-up your team?"

- I've already been on the phone. I think three days should do it.

- The guns and the machine gun?

- Already found. They can be in Key Largo tomorrow if needed.

- Great. What about the boat?

- Craig says that he can be here tomorrow morning in his private jet plane if this is a go. We can all fly back with him to Key Largo.

- OK. We can use the time you need to familiarize ourselves with the boat and the guns.

- Craig is willing to spend some time with you to show you how to run the boat. What about the crew?

- I forgot to ask, but I think not. There is another thing. You need a trigger to start your thing. While you must start your investigation of the GV organization right away, you have to wait on your thing until we have Michelle or you don't hear from us after a number of hours past the start of our end. Here is what I think, I can call you on the satellite phone and simply tell you: 'How are you doing?' That is your clue to start on GV. You need to reply: 'Not bad.' That is all we need to say. When you hear this, you will take Michelle's husband and kid to a secure location and start your operation. On the other hand, if you don't hear from us in ten hours after we start-off from the mooring, you start as if we had called you. Does that make sense?

- Got it. I will call you when Craig arrives and we can go to the bank to take care of business. Are you sure that you don't want two or three of my guys to go with you?

- I am not sure of anything at this time, but the answer is no. I'm beat. I'm off to bed. See you in the morning.

Meeting Craig and going to the bank went very well. They drove to the airport and got in the Lear jet to fly back to the keys believing that they were in the clear, but minor things can escalate. To fly from Grand

Cayman to Florida, one either flies over Cuba or takes a radical left going west only to revert back northeast to reach Florida. But the Cubans do allow flyovers with permits. Even private planes can fly over if the pilot is the owner of the plane and requests and receives a permit in a timely fashion. Most pilots request the permit to avoid the much longer flight. This is what Craig opted to do when he flew to Grand Cayman from the keys. Unfortunately, and inadvertently, he requested a one-way flight, forgetting to incorporate the return flight on the permit. The Lear jet soon finds itself in Cuba's territorial waters without a permit to fly over Cuba.

Elizabeth, always curious about Cuba and its people, sits at the co-pilot chair when the Cuban Mig approaches the Lear jet, flying to its left, and signals that he wants the Lear to follow him down to land. Soon, over the radio, comes the command:

- You are flying over Cuba without a permit. Follow me to the Cienfuegos airport. You will land there.

- What is happening, Craig? -, says Elizabeth.

- I don't know. I have a permit. Don't worry. It is just a mix-up. We'll be alright.

He's a stout man, about 5' 10" with thinning white hair, a white heavy mustache, a very light skin, and a deep voice that sometimes quivers. He turns-on the passenger message radio and announces:

- We're going to make a short stop in Cienfuegos. There's no reason to be alarmed. I just have to clarify some paperwork with the Cuban authorities. We'll be back in the air in no time.

But Bill worries. He experienced some confrontations with Cuban government agents in the past, and he worries that Cuban authorities recognize and detain him in Cuba. John and Jorge took Craig at his word and welcome the experience to be in Cuba if only for a couple of hours.

They receive landing instructions, land, and receive instructions to follow a truck to a hangar where they enter, stop the Lear jet, and shot it down. As they exit the plane, they see armed soldiers waiting for them. The soldiers escort them to an office where they provide identifications.

Craig shows the officer his permit and says:

- As you see officer Cintron, I have a permit. I would appreciate that you allow us to return to our flight as quickly as possible, sir.

Captain Cintron replies, - This permit is to fly from Florida to Grand Cayman over Cuba. It does not allow you to fly from Grand Cayman to Florida over Cuba. You and your passengers need to go to the waiting room while I contact my commanding officer.

- But sir, ...

- If you cannot do as I say voluntarily, I can have my soldiers force you. What will it be?

- No, sir. We'll go.

Flying over Cuba without a permit can result in just a heavy fine. But once you are within the jurisdiction of Cuban authorities, other things may apply, and you are at their mercy. Pictures and fingerprints later, they all sit in the waiting room, and Craig offers,

- It's a foul-up. They say I did not have permit for the return to Florida flight, but don't worry. They will give me a fine, and we'll be back on our way soon.

- I hope so -, says Jorge.

- Amen -, chimes John.

- Are getting religious on me? -, chides Elizabeth.

- Just saying.

They wait uneasily for three hours until Captain Cintron walks-in and says:

- Miss Parker, you will come with me.

- Wait a minute -, says John -, why just her? What about us? Can I go with her?

- Just sit down and wait -, says the captain sternly.

- I'll be all right, John. Do as he says.

Elizabeth follows Cintron down the aisle, out of the hanger, into a jeep and they drive off.

- May I ask where we're going?

- To my commanding officer's headquarters. It's not far.

They arrive at an old cement building in need of repairs and a paint job. Elizabeth follows Cintron to a first-floor office where a clerk tells them to go right in.

- Captain Cintron reporting, as ordered, sir.

- Thank you, Captain. Please wait outside.

- Yes, sir.

As he leaves, General Cisneros tells Elizabeth,

- Please sit down.

- I'm a bit confused, General. What can I do for you?

- Elizabeth, may I call you Elizabeth.

- Yes, sir.

The short man appeared to be in his sixties or seventies. He is slim, his face shows age, but his presence commands attention.

- Let me tell you a story, Elizabeth. In June of 1960, after the ridiculous and treacherous invasion of the United States in the Bay of Pigs, a major demonstration took place in Washington, DC, condemning the invasion and demanding that the United States stay away from the affairs of Cuba and other independent countries. A number of the demonstrators were arrested. The news coverage captures a very young, small, frail, and beautiful redheaded woman struggling against a soldier trying to get her under control. I was an eighteen-year-old soldier at the time. I saw the flash of the red hair and those fiery green eyes, and I fell immediately in love with that woman. As sometimes happens, I kept that memory alive all these years. Investigations through the years uncovered a name: Elizabeth Parker. Can you imagine my surprise when Captain Cintron tells me that among a group of detainees was a redheaded woman called Elizabeth Parker? The picture confirmed my suspicions. What are you doing with a known paramilitary person, an ex-military intelligence person, and that man called John? Are you the same woman?

- That was another place, another time. But, yes. It was me. How could you possibly be impressed by and remember after so many years what must have been a very short news clip?

- Like I said, I remembered, but please answer my question. What are you doing with these people?

- John is my husband. I guess you mean Jorge when you speak of military intelligence.

- That's right, but how do you know?

- We used to be married.

- I see. What about Jorge?

- He knows no secrets. He was just a linguist-typist with a very low security clearance.

- And Bill?

- We were young. He was a kind of revel at the time. We became friends.

- You did not marry this one?

- No. We were just friends.

- And Craig?

- He's Bill's friend. I just met him.

- All right. What are all of you up to?

Staring into his eyes, Elizabeth knew that if she lied, the man would know, and if she told him the truth, he would have a hard time believing her, so she shed a tear or two to have time to think.

- Come now, you can tell me.

Because she knew she could not get away with lying, she told him.

- That is some story. Nobody could make this up. And did you already notify these people of your plans?

- Yes.

- I see. Here's what we're going to do. Your pilot is in for a mayor fine, but I am going to let all of you go. Here is my card. If you run into trouble near our waters, I want you to call me. I'll try to help. And if you come out of this alive, I would like you to visit Cuba as my guest anytime you wish.

- I don't know what to say except thank you, sir.

- Just remember me and Cuba. Come visit sometime.

- I would really like that, sir.

- Very well.

And the captain took her back, Craig paid a $10,000 fine and they were off again.

Sitting side by side, John asks Elizabeth, "What happened?"

And since she never lied to him, she told him.

- Wow.

- Yes.

Tired from the stress and the flight, nothing much was said as they flew on to the keys.

....

As it was, they found a spare marine GPS that was similar to the one installed in the control room. They plugged it in and it was soon working. Michelle found the satellite phone where it had dropped, in a corner of the control room. Jorge called Bill. And they reset their course based on the existing coordinates.

- John, how are we going to manage to throw the machine gun over the side? That thing is heavy.

- Yes, and we have to remove the holding bolts and finish this before the Coast Guard sees us. There is nothing to do but start the job and see. Where are the tools?

- Right here, under this cover. I'll get them.

- Just get what we need out of that chest. It's too heavy to carry the whole thing.

- Right -, says Jorge selecting an adjustable wrench, a few ½" sockets, an extension, and a ratchet.

- Let's go.

- You stay. I'll do it. Give me that line.

- I'll come along in case you need help, Superman -, Jorge says giving half the tools to John and carrying the rope.

And it was a good thing they were both there. They barely managed to remove the machine gun, tie it to the line and lower it to the main deck. From there, they pushed it by the side.

- What about the guns? -, asks Jorge -, and by the way, where did you get that 45 canon?

- It's always been my preferred gun. I asked Bill to get it for me. He had one of his men pick it up from my son's house and bring it to Key West. I am most comfortable shooting it. With our lives on the line, I had to have my own gun. Besides Bill says that the other guns are not legally registered, and so the only gun that it is legal to have on board is my gun. We need to toss all the other guns overboard.

- Right. Then there is not much we can do until we meet the Hamilton. Hey, you're bleeding again.

- Yeah. You too. Let's see Kelly. She'll be happy to see this.

So, a few drops of blood here and there? No problem. They got rid of the other guns. They had their story straight. Some unknown people kidnapped Michelle and ordered them to meet them in the high seas without informing the police. They did as they were told but the exchange went bad because they did not have the ransom money and they had to shoot the two men that were on the deck. The boat was still registered to Craig, who had lent it to them so that they could go fishing. They somehow eluded a boat that followed them when inexplicably it blew-up behind them. It was hard to tell if the Coast Guard people believed their story, but it would be hard to find any evidence to the contrary since they could not pinpoint the locations of the events described. At any rate, the events had occurred in international waters where the Coast Guard had no jurisdiction, and when they met the Hamilton, there was nothing illegal in their boat or persons.

Kelly was just unfortunate enough to be in the wrong place at the wrong time. The GV people kidnapped her and brought her with them in case they needed medical assistance. She said she knew nothing, and she was probably saying the truth.

Hours later, when they arrived at Key West, Jorge called Bill.

- Hi.

- How's it going?

- Fine. You?

- In Key West.

- I'll call you back in a couple of hours. Still have some stuff to do. When I am done, I'll come down to meet you.

- Later.

Facts are often stranger than fiction. No way are these events believable. Bill told Jorge that the operation went very well. Twenty-seven people had disappeared without explanation. Two of his own men died. The operation captured 553 million dollars in its asset recovery portion.

- What do you want me to do with the money?

- It belongs to you and your men.

- We don't operate in that scale. The agreement is 50K for each man. I think 50K more as a bonus would more than suffice for us. What do you want me to do with the rest?

- Put it in that account we set-up for you. I have the password. Hire a person to manage this as an insurance account. As a matter of fact, set-up a registered insurance company in some country that can legally pay funds to people at a time of need. Tell your people that we have set-up a fun to care for any problems they face in the future that require money. All any of them has to do is call the person you hire and it will be taken care of.

- I never heard of any such thing.

- It's only money, and we have not earned any of it. You and your men did.

- I need to let you know that me and my people (when they hear about this, I am sure) will go anywhere and do anything you ask.

- I appreciate that. We have a fund of nearly one billion dollars. We might be able to do some good things with that money. I will discuss it with Elizabeth and John to see if they have any ideas. But really, we could not have done any of this without your help. I want you to know that we appreciate everything you did.

A shake of the hands, a brief embrace, and Bill is off. Jorge turns to join Elizabeth and John at the Casa Marina, Waldorf Astoria Resort.

- Hey guys. You're still here, Kelly?

- I could not leave without thanking you.

- You're welcome, but I think you need to thank the universe, God, or whomever you believe in. We did some crazy things that should never have turned out the way they did. So, some external force may have been helping us. Have a good life, Kelly, and thanks for patching us up.

- You're welcome. Bye.

A chorus of byes led her to the door and back to her life.

- What about Bill? -, Elizabeth asks.

- Interesting situation. Nobody is going to be bothering you again from the GV people. I won't say any more about that, but we have an interesting situation that we need to address. It's the money. Not only do we have more than 400 million in the first accounts, Bill captured more than 500 million in an asset recovery action I asked him to perform. What do you want to do with this money?

- What the hell! I don't think we want any part of this. It's enough we have to explain the luxurious living we've had the last few days. How do we explain that other money? -, says John.

- I am not sure what to do about this. What do you have in mind, Jorge? -, says Elizabeth.

- I understand you, John. Believe me. I do. But we can't just ignore this. It won't go away. Besides, I don't see how a numbered account is going to track back to you. The important thing is to find a way to use the money in a positive way that does not affect your income tax finances."

- How do you mean?"

- If we create an international corporation based in Grand Cayman and allocate some of the funds we have here to the corporation, and we also create an entity in the US to receive funding from the Grand Cayman corporation, we can use the money in a legal way to do some of the things that are important to both of you.

- Like helping needy students pay their university tuition? -, says Elizabeth.

- If that's what you want, you can create a nonprofit for that with funding from the GC corporation.

- Or funding promising young composers? -, says John.

- Another nonprofit. Yes.

- What would you want to do? -, asks John.

- I'm thinking about that. I'm not ready to say yet. I think each of us can come up with worthwhile projects we can pursue, and there's enough money for many, many projects.

- Will you be using Bill again in some of your ideas? -, asks Elizabeth.

- I don't reject that possibility, but if I do, I will not involve you except to request permission to access the funding. Nearly half of all the money is in the account we created to pay Bill. The other half, only you have access. If you prefer, we can agree to a complete and permanent separation of the funds so that you can do your thing, and I can do mine.

- I like that -, says John.

- All right then. That's what we'll do, Jorge -, says Elizabeth.

And so, with a parting of the ways, friends went about doing what they could to improve the world as they saw fit. One set within the system, the other not necessarily. Their sleepless nights ended with a new dawn that opened their lives to many new possibilities.

Engraved Memories

After seventy years you ask,

- When did love first arrive to that timid and sensitive boy? An easier question to answer would be, when did you first feel the heat of the sun? Making this question more difficult is my confusion between sex and love (which existed and exists in my life). Because I wanted to have idealistic relationships remaining my timid self before the passions that stormed about me then and still do now, my relationships were not then nor are they now those expected from a passionate Latin man, although I spent a year at twenty-six having sexual relations every day getting drunk and doing everything one could do in search of mundane pleasures. Fury and vengeance? To your question, I don't know, but let me reduce the theme of my first love to a fleeting moment.

Images floating above dancing waves,

between palm fronds and the salt of the sea,

in inscrutable memory: inerasable memories

of lost illusions that will never die

and that unexpectedly, and at times disguised,

sometimes resurface demanding attention

- Rio Piedras was perhaps the second largest town in the island. It is the site of the University of Puerto Rico. The town had its own city government, baseball and basketball teams. What a pity! The expansion of San Juan swallowed it.

- In the enormous rear patio of that two-story, flat-roofed structure equally enormous with all that cement, my mother, two brothers and I lived in aunt Juana's house. A band of kids played baseball and basketball there between the plants, the trees, and atop the bare ground where I once while running barefoot gashed a foot on the bottom of a broken glass bottle. The sun and humidity made sweat run everywhere.

- I don't remember how I met her there. We were about ten or twelve. Her black eyes sparked mischievous glances everywhere above rose-scarlet lips that appeared to beg for kisses. Her pale, clear-skin face floated within a frame of black, shiny, curvilinear hair. Her body insinuated that of a woman. I ask myself now, "How could that girl have had that sensual walk?"

- I spoke of love to her, I wrote her poems, I spent long hours at her house (around the corner), and when she went to New York, I wrote her letters. Truly, I was a puppy dog following her around.

I never pulled her to me to embrace or to kiss her.

- Perhaps because of that, below a brilliant sun, atop warm and tan sands in a Puertorican beach, close to the waving fronds of palm trees, many years later, when a friend introduced me to that beautiful smiling North American woman, clad in a blue bikini that contrasted with the many colors of the sea, instead of offering her my hand, I pulled her to me, gave her a fierce embrace, and kissed her passionately on her lips. She was startled but not offended, and kissed me straight back.

But it was way too late.

To Cities Around the Bay

We met at my house, and my buddy, his girlfriend and I took an Uber to the airport. The flight from Las Vegas to San Francisco was uneventful.

The drive from SFO to Fisherman's Wharf took us through near downtown, past Chinatown where one could walk the sidewalks and gaze at the myriad vendor items placed behind glass to entice tourists to empty their wallets, past the then dormant symphony hall that stages music I sometimes long for, near the AT&T stadium where the San Francisco Giants recently fell to their eleventh straight loss and where I once took my family during a work day when a secretary called to find out where I was and asked me to return to the office, and I did not return, near the San Francisco-Oakland Bay bridge, which survives the daily awe of tourists to the more famous Golden Gate Bridge, over some steep hills, which one drives-up only to gasp at the straight-down drop on the other side, and the "curviest street in the world," which is no more than a one and a half city blocks of zig zags down a hill, past slow-moving street-trolleys filled with people hanging-on to its sides, and finally to the covered parking one has to reserve in advance to ensure that one does not waste time finding where to park and paying a fortune to park near the Fisherman's Wharf when one's agenda is so tight that there is no time to see all the attractions in the city because visiting San Francisco like this is like passing through the first room at the Prado and rushing off to others things because there is no time. No time to linger at Pier 39 gazing at the sea lions resting in the man-made floats. They bark occasionally and scratch their skins with their flips from time to time never paying heed to the onlookers that take picture after picture as if they could keep this memory that way and no time to see the wares of the stores that offer all kinds of trinkets so that the visitors can try to take something of the wonder they saw not realizing that they keep the memory through the years, or they do not.

The world knows the San Francisco Bay, but it belongs to more than just San Francisco. Many communities surround the bay to the south, the east and the north. That is why for locals, it is the Bay Area where I went with a group of friends trolling for salmon. The woman captain caught one beautiful specimen of which I received a wonderful boneless share. One can cook a salmon, but it's better to eat it raw with a bit of lemon juice.

One eats at a restaurant at the wharf because it is part of the experience paying for the overpriced food like all the other tourists who yearn to partake of the famous items in the menu not caring that it will soon go to waste in one way or another, and one rushes on to the Golden Gate because one cannot go to San Francisco without passing through that bridge, and stops at the north side to gaze at the bridge and take pictures—for one most take pictures. Going north, one leaves Sausalito behind with the finer restaurants like the Spinnaker—which lies at the waterfront in Sausalito where I was tempted to buy a property in one of those hills overlooking the bay until I found out that very cold winds rise from the bay that often make it unbearable to be outside in those hills—where if one does spend a lot for a cioppino, one does it in a fine atmosphere in comfort and with a fine view, but there is no time, and one goes on to the majestic redwoods at Muir Woods because there are some things one cannot miss, and this is one of them: to stand near a tree that requires a number of people holding hands making a circle to cover its girth and that rises over three-hundred and fifty feet without one being able to see beyond thirty or forty feet above one's head because the limbs hide the heights to which these giants rise. They say that these trees grow a foot per year. The equivalence of several frail-human lifetimes they grew to their current height. But one cannot stay for long because the vineyards of Napa Valley await to give you free tastes of the wine produced in this area of lazy sloping hills painted with greens and the occasional man-made structure that seems out of place, and one just wants the vineyards and the wine tasting without human interference, but you spent too much time in other things, the drive to Napa through heavy traffic, and the wine tasting this holiday weekend does not materialize.

So, on you drive to Sacramento and find the old city historic district where one can see both the old train and the Delta King Hotel composed of an old stern-wheel river boat that now rests unable to move on its own because it surrendered its engine to another river boat—perhaps the Fort Lauderdale River Queen, which cruises (their owners say: majestically) along the New River that flows from the Everglades to the many waters of Fort Lauderdale—allowing visitors to spend nights aboard, eat at its restaurant, have drinks at its bar, or just sit by one of its "barandas" perhaps drinking coffee and being transported to another place in another time, even transformed to another person living another age, but you are tired now from the flight from LAS to SFO, the drive to many places and the walks through these tourists destinations, and you just want to find your hotel and rest through the night because the next day has another very busy agenda.

Although one can drive straight through from Sacramento to Lake Tahoe, ours was not a race but a discovery experience, so we diverted from I80 to Hwy 49 and took a look at Nevada City, which I mistook for Virginia City at the other side of the Nevada border, and that was a fortunate mistake because in the trip we enjoyed views of the Sierra Nevada along our way before we found old Nevada City with its preserved mining iron works, a well preserved architecture, and the charm of its people that made us welcome. We had lunch at the Sopa Thai Cuisine that hides in its interior a large outdoor patio where one can commune with other visitors and locals under the shade of the large centerpiece tree or by the raised patio attached to the restaurant building where we learned from a local that one should stay in the city a while to walk along the irrigation ditches and enjoy the incredible flora and fauna of this place. No time, but lunch was fantastic, and we did a wine tasting of sorts in a store along the side of a main street before taking the road towards Truckee.

It's hard to say why my companions liked Truckee so much. As a town it is just a few streets that support the winter ski resorts that create a demand for housing that raises their prices so exorbitantly that locals cannot afford to live here. How can they be locals if they don't live here? My companions loved the winter lodges along the ridges that serve as a backdrop to the small community, but for me, it is its nearness to the Donner Lake and the Alder Creek Valley, which the Donner Party made famous, or perhaps one might say, infamous in their struggles to cross the Sierra in the middle of a terrible winter that makes this town interesting. We did have an excellent coffee at the Dark Horse Coffee Roasters where we met a beautiful slim young woman who told us how she and her husband, who is a building contractor, were fortunate enough to purchase a small fixer-upper for two-hundred and fifty thousand dollars, and they were in the process of fixing it. So on to Reno, but before we simply had to stop at Donner Lake to take pictures in the dwindling light of a marvelous sunset.

But we drive-on to Carson City in search of our hotel and our beds to bathe and to rest until the morrow. And we do find it, but when I ask for my two-room reservation, but they can only find one room under my name, and we ask them to talk to Hotel.com, and I show them my confirmation, and they make calls, and I make calls, and all of a sudden, after many minutes of this, I mention my partner's name, and one of the hotel desk clerks says they do have a reservation under that name, so we finally get our rooms and head for them all stressed-out, but after a while my friends call me to say they want to go do karaoke at Reno, and we take off for a Mexican restaurant where they might have karaoke, and they do for about an hour, but the man doing the karaoke who is dressed in Mariachi attire and has a charming smile has to take off for two hours, and because I gave my business card to the owner, they ask me to take over the show for the two hours the man has to be away, but it is not my karaoke machine nor my operating software, and I tell them that I probably would not do it well because of this, but they insist telling that they will pay me, and so I do what I can with numerous errors in a place full of nearly drunk singers that want to know what is the matter with me, and finally the regular karaoke guy returns, and we leave shortly thereafter to return to Carson City where I dive onto the bed and sleep.

We do better the next morning arriving at the breakfast place in the hotel before breakfast is over and we sit at a round table with other guests to eat and drink and talk about where we come from, where we've been, and where we are going. Nice people. Most people on vacation are nice. We load our suitcases in the car and take off for Virginia City with me hoping to buy another belt buckle in the same place where I bought the one I bought there years ago when I went there with my son Carlos who corrected me when I said I bought it in Nevada City where we never visited and I search the streets for the place where I bought it to no avail. Many stores had buckles but not like mine all shiny looking more like white gold than stainless steel, relatively large, and with a center place to place a silver dollar as a center piece. We walked the street and stopped at a couple of stores before we headed out to Lake Tahoe where we had to wait a long time to park the car because there was no parking space and then wait standing in line at the pier to enter the large lake ship that would take us on a cruise in the lake. At each side of the pier children played in the transparent waters of the shallows while others floated here and there, paddled four-people water bicycles, or just lay on the sandy shore looking toward the calm waters of the bay which often display sun made floating, sparkling diamonds.

While my buddy and his girlfriend sit on a bench enjoying the trip, I wrestle with creating a place for myself in this trip that I agreed to take to be their guide, at their expense, and wonder if I made their trip worthwhile. There is nothing more than water, shoreline and a man giving details of the history of the lake in the excursion as if the onlookers cared, or even heard what he said, but the river craft was steady, and no one felt dizzy, and it was over soon enough.

The trip, we felt, was essentially over, and we drove to the Reno airport to determine the length of the trip there, decided to find a nearby coffee place to burn some time until we had to check-in, and the coffee at a nearby Starbucks was good. We left early enough to drop-off the rented car and check-in at the Allegiant counter where a woman told us that we had to pay five dollars each to get our boarding passes, but that she did not guarantee that we could catch our plane even though we were forty-five minutes before flight time, and when we arrive at the gate, the Allegiant rep told us that we could not board, and there we were without a plane to fly us back to Las Vegas, with no other flight until morning—and that flight would cost us over two-hundred dollars each—and if we decided to take the afternoon Allegiant flight, it would cost us seventy five dollars each when the original flight cost was only eighty-one dollars. It was surprising that no one boiled over, but it was close. It took the cool mind of my friend to find the obvious answer: rent a car and drive to Las Vegas. I negotiated the rental of a full-size car for a reasonable price and offered to drive the seven hours back to Vegas. My buddy's girlfriend was worried that I would be too tired to drive safely, and when the GPS took us East instead of South, my friends wondered if we were going in the right direction. There are no freeways most of the way. As we drove from one small town to another on two-way, one-lane each way, country roads, she sat by my side either singing, asking me to sing, speaking, or asking me to speak to ensure that I would stay awake and alert. I followed her lead to make sure that she did not stress out more that she already was while my buddy sat in the back seat checking the photos he took on the trip without paying much attention to the doings in the front seat. We stopped at a Tonopah casino and drank coffee before getting back on the road, and we arrived at my house—

where they had left their car—about eight hours after we left Reno. They took their suitcases and left. In the afternoon, we returned the rental car. One might say that I was dead in the morning, but I felt better in the afternoon. From wake-up call on Friday at 5AM until the arrival at my house at 7AM on Monday, 74 hours passed, we drove nearly 900 miles, and we slept about 14 hours. It was a trip.

Serious and not so Serious Writings

After the Long Ride to the West

around the south side and the return around the north side and the nights with little sleep:

Incoming lights glare as I follow the white right-line that guides the wheels of the car rolling somewhat unsure on the asphalt speckled with holes that suddenly appear and jar the weary journey. Wipers try their best to clear the glass.

There was a bridge on the trip that I passed unaware of its presence. I knew it was part of the journey, but I do not remember the passing. I do remember wondering when and if it would come, or if it was left behind.

I stopped to drink a coffee at a roadside cafe, and as I sat facing the entrance, the sun brought in the day. Soon, a few more miles, and beyond the up- and down-sloping curves: home at a little house atop a lonesome hill.

The View From my Window

The view outside my window has not changed over the years. Many flowers, giant fern, banana, plantain, and coconut trees amongst bushes and grasses create a lively green vista—nearly always the same. The house hundreds of feet directly in front does dress differently with each holiday. That is all.

Deep down I may have resented that. Perhaps like a Spanish-song claims, even beauty can become boring. I guess it may be the training we in receive of minute videos that train the brain to the expectation of constant change.

But opening the window to such beauty cannot be the same as going from channel to channel on TV. One must adjust the brain, as one adjusts so many controls, to control unreasonable expectations. If one eliminates such things, the never-ending view from the window retains its value. Someone should look at creating adjustments (controls) over our expectations. I will try to control mine. Expectations slur the way we see and value our daily lives. That aside, I will forever love the view from my window atop the small hill within the glorious mountain chain of my beloved Puerto Rico.

Of Roosters and Others

A riot of roosters of gold, reds and blacks roam the country road unsure of their best route to go to find wherever food and hens are found. Too late for crowing and too early for roosting, they walk the sometimes hot and sometimes cold tar beneath their feet coming here and going there not knowing where to go or when they are there.

Hence, it is mostly the hens that pull them, and they go uneasily wondering which others they might have to face to gain a hen. A simple life one might posit, but for them it is all they know and all they have. And so, they live it.

I wonder how many share a rooster's fate.

What Will Be

The road winds by the desert mountains

Bereft of the missed greens

Off to the right a lake dies

Overused by the growing spans

Of never-ending dwellings

Of ever-growing place

Thoughts wander in space

That drops and rises by flood zones

Time passes through the road

That leads to the unknown

What will time bring?

From Our Verandah

From our verandah, often fog-covered mountains surround the limits of our world; a world we only begin to know by bits and pieces for we just came from another world: dried and almost bereft of the wonders of rain, plants and trees that fill this new world. But we are condemned to wait another day to learn more, as a foreign virus that tries to conquer what we thought was an ordered and somewhat safe civilization restricts us from leaving our home.

Much separated what we thought we could do from what we actually did, but our thoughts were pleasant consolations that eased the strains caused by the changes in our lives. The friends and relatives left behind created a hole we tried to fill with new people, but, for now, we felt them wanting and unable to fill that stressing void.

Drives around roads spread views of wondrous mountain chains, valleys of green, and to the distant horizon: the seemingly unending sea. White and grey clouds filed the sky with only patches of bright blue interrupting their formations.

In the midst of this, houses too small for human habitation dotted some of the lands, but we knew they were bigger than they seemed. When approached, most of those houses were newly painted and well cared for. Many of them we might have entertained having as our home; although, our own pretty house atop our pleasant hill was a very good choice among them all.

We are left with the need to manage the other clouds that inhabit our minds. We must deal with the doubts, fears, should and would haves in this new uncertain and uncontrollable world. The other seemingly neater world we left behind does not exist anymore, but we long for it without logic or reason.

Outside our windows, birds chirp, a bright sun warms the land; and trees, plants of roses and other flowers cover the ground. Perhaps we shall take a few steps around and about this place we call our home and be part of it all.

Routines

A cool breeze lifts the wings of curtains of the far window. This chilling August air, in this early morning, atop this hill that is embraced by the central mountain chain of this Caribbean island, chides the waiting summer heat, caresses me, and flees the room by the window next to me. Too soon, it dissipates.

Sunlight filters through a mantle of clouds. Perhaps last night's thunders shy the sun, but it will pull through sometime. Perhaps. Perhaps the threatening storm will bypass us.

But what will become of us left, as we are, enclosed in our home with few places to go to and few people to see.

Outside, a small dog barks at some unwelcome sight. Does it think that its barks will take away that thing that bothers him? Are these barks like the screams some people make when they are frightened by some unwelcome thing that disrupts their comfortable routines? Do they think that their screams will take that thing away?

And yet, to break away from a routine is sometimes welcome.

Outside, the men repairing the downed fiber optic cable continue their work. They will return the good internet to replace the troublesome excuse we are using now.

That will be something.

Vocabulary

Word Meaning

Abuela Grandmother

Amapolas Red poppies

Canita Literally "little cane." Rum illegally made at home.

Chiva Literally "goat." A shutout in a domino game.

Dita Gourd

Guaraguao Red-tailed hawk of Puerto Rico and Cuba

Madrina Godmother

Mami Mommy

Nene Boy

Papi Daddy

Pava Straw hat

Paso fino Literally "fine step." Mule gait preferred by land owners

Reinitas Literally "little queens." A Puertorican black and yellow bird.

Roca Rock

Titi Aunty

Tio Uncle

Yuca Cassava

www.ingramcontent.com/pod-product-compliance
Lightning Source LLC
LaVergne TN
LVHW012103160826
845678LV00014B/2913

* 9 7 9 8 3 6 4 3 0 0 8 4 3 *